SOUTH
OF
BAGHDAD

STEVEN CHARLES

$16.00 USD

STEVEN CHARLES

STARS IN THE WIND

THE MAN IN BLUE

SOUTH OF BAGHDAD

AMERICA:
Practical Solutions For The 21st Century

DANCINGGROUNDENTERTAINMENT@GMAIL.COM

Cast of Characters

Emmy Sebastian - an airline stewardess

Dante Sebastian - Emmy's father, a Las Vegas chef

Stephanie Granger - a hotel executive

Mark Sebastian - a young USMC recruit

Angelo Cicci - Mark's brazen USMC pal

Uncle Ray - a retired Marine

Carmen Sebastian - Emmy and Mark's mother

Hilario "Larry" Valdespino - a young USMCrecruit

James "Wichita" Sykes - a young USMC recruit

Oliver Ralston - a very loud USMC First Sergeant

Captain Dylan - a USMC commanding officer

Caressa Rose - Captain Dylan's fiancee

Dudley - Dante's sous chef at the hotel

Diana Scott - host of Three Voices show

Wayne Ballantree - a Democratic Congressman

Fitzpatrick Pynchon - a retired Army general

Kassim Al Khayyam - an Arab journalist

Marcus Sebastian - Dante's father, a retired Marine

Flo - Marcus' favorite nurse

Frank Cicci - Angelo's father, a Chicago mortician

Terri Anthony - Mark's surprising new love interest

Estelle Cantrell - mother of a wounded Marine

January 2003

At fifteen minutes before midnight the Las Vegas hotel casino was packed full of extremely boisterous guests. Still dressed in her stewardess uniform, Emmy Sebastian plowed her way through the unruly crowd as diplomatically as possible.

"No, I will not kiss you!" she exclaimed to an inebriated guest who attempted to grab her. "It's not even midnight, and you're definitely not my type."

She forced her way through the celebratory crowd toward the private banquet rooms. A guard by the banquet room recognized her.

"Good evening, Miss Sebastian."

She nodded her thanks and hurried inside. Emmy was immediately relieved to see her smiling father dressed in his crisp white chef's uniform.

"Honey, what took you so long?"

"Dad, I'm lucky I even got here! Flight delays, security hassles, extremely drunk passengers, and bad weather the whole way," she explained as they hugged.

"Just the usual routine then?"

"Exactly!"

A tall, very attractive brunette in a business suit walked up to join them.

"Emmy, this is Stephanie Granger, " smiled her father, "Director of Catering for the hotel."

"Did our driver find you all right?" asked Stephanie while shaking hands with Emmy.

"Yes, and thank you," replied Emmy. "I felt a little guilty having him wait all that time. I know you have much more important guests than me."

"There are no more important guests than our Executive Chef's daughter. If you'll excuse me, unlike some of our staff," she informed Emmy while nudging her father in a rather friendly way, "I am still working. But I hope to see both of you later."

Stephanie hurried off and Emmy quickly gauged the look on her father's face as he enjoyed watching her disappear back onto the casino floor.

"She's beautiful, Dad."

"Yes, I noticed that too."

"She's also about half your age."

"Well, not quite. Is that a problem, daughter who never misses anything?"

"Not a problem for me if it's not for you two. Where's Mark? Is Mom here?"

"Everyone is out on the terrace to watch the fireworks. First, let's get us both a drink," he suggested, grabbing two glasses of champagne off a tray, "and get it this year over with."

Father and daughter hurried out the French doors onto the cool terrace where a very libation friendly group awaited. Aunt Jeannie was the first to see Emmy, letting out a yell as she spilled her drink on Uncle Ray and then squealed over to hug her. When dark-haired Carmen Sebastian saw her daughter she reacted like an airplane had been pulled out of a monkey's mouth in a Las Vegas magical act as she pushed new husband Herb aside and hurried over to embrace her daughter.

Uncle Ray and Herb led the greeting line of cousins, family friends, and even her father's Sous Chef Dudley, still in uniform.

Finally, there was nothing to separate Emmy from her tall younger brother Mark in his Marine uniform and looking as handsome as she had ever seen him. They hugged for a long time, then Emmy smiled at Mark with tears in her eyes.

"You're always late, Sis, but somehow you're always still just in time."

Mark waved his beer bottle towards a shorter, obviously Italian Marine leering at her.

"Emmy, this is my buddy Angelo Cicci. We ran into each other during basic training and surprisingly haven't killed each other yet."

"Angelo, it's a pleasure."

"Miss Emmy," replied Angelo, reaching down to softly kiss her hand, "pleasure is the name of my game, and don't you ever forget it."

"Angelo!" Mark warned with a sharp elbow.

"Sorry," Angelo half-heartedly apologized. "I did promise your brother I wouldn't hit on you but it may be almost impossible not to. It's a second nature thing, you know what I mean?"

"No, I don't think I do."

"*Cheech*?" inquired Uncle Ray, more than a bit tipsy. "Is that like in Cheech and Chong?"

"No," responded Angelo in a less condescending tone than possible, "it's like the Cicci family of funeral parlor operators in the greater Chicago area. Cheech and Chong? My last name is spelled C-i-c-c-i, which reads like *Chee-Chee* but is actually pronounced *Cheech*."

"I was the only guy in our unit Angelo couldn't seem to manipulate. He was so confused when his usual methods for working people didn't work on me," Mark explained to his sister as he reached for another beer, "I felt sorry and took the ugly little mutt under my wing."

"Little mutt?" scowled Angelo. "Shark, I'm a Devil Dog, and don't you freaking forget it!"

"What unit are you guys in?" asked Uncle Ray, puffing out his chest.

"We're presently in a Force Service Support Group," replied Mark. "That's all we're allowed to say. We won't be the first unit going into Iraq, but we'll be very close behind all those that do."

"We have been told to expect some pretty heavy shit, which is cool," added Angelo.

"You probably know, I was a Marine too," Uncle Ray reminded anyone who didn't know. "In Vietnam from '69 to '71. It was a rough go, but that's why they sent in Marines. I don't like having my nephew to go over there and fight, but there's no question we have to stop Saddam Hussein and Osama bin Laden from hitting us with all those damn weapons of mass destruction."

A nearly unanimous cheer went up in response to Uncle Ray's impassioned plea. Glasses met in toast and even more alcohol was consumed. There was only one low voice of dissent.

"Even if it means completely ignoring the United Nations and making a pre-emptive strike without any firm evidence?" inquired Dante.

"The bottom line for us," explained Mark in a loud voice, "is nothing matters except the job we have to go over and do. Marines are going to kick major ass in Iraq, and that is how it works."

"Amen to that!" agreed Uncle Ray. "When do you boys leave for Camp Pendleton?"

"*We Marines*," Angelo corrected, "have to report by the fourteenth of January. The way it looks right now, we'll be headed to Kuwait around the end of the month. As far as Iraq, who knows?"

"Well, we're behind you 110%!" said Uncle Ray, speaking for everyone.

Dante raised a glass to Mark with certainty.

"Absolutely! Support our troops, if not the poor ill-advised bastards who put them there."

"Exactly!" echoed Emmy while checking her watch. "Come on, it's almost time."

The countdown chant to New Years was beginning and soon one tumultuous year would pass over into the uncertainty of the next. Music began playing and a thunderous, very colorful fireworks display exploded over the Las Vegas Strip. Everyone kissed everyone else and then watched the fireworks display. Emmy stood between brother and father.

"Mark, do me a favor?" asked Dante.

"Yes Sir, of course."

"Number one, when you call me Sir it makes me feel older than I really am, so please just call me Dad like always. Secondly, promise me you'll be right back here with us next year, same time, same place."

Mark thought about it for a second and then leaned over to kiss his sister on the forehead.

"I will make and keep that promise."

*   *   *

Emmy and Mark were having lunch at a lodge on Mt. Charleston with a worried mother Carmen.

"Mom, don't worry. I'll be alright."

"Is that what they tell you to tell us?"

"Yes, the whole thing is a big conspiracy of lies. And to think I always thought you and Dad weren't on the same page about anything?"

"We really do agree about one important thing," his mother pointed out, "and that is about wanting you to stay alive. I wish I could be in San Diego with you when you leave, but-"

"Not a problem, Mom. I really won't mind not leaving my Marines this image of my mother sending me off to war like it's the first day of school."

"Will you be having a girl there to see you off?" asked Carmen hopefully.

"Not unless I get lucky real soon. Since I broke up with Christy I haven't been in a hurry to get serious with anyone. Lots of guys are marrying up before they leave so they have something to come back to, but I think whether or not you come back is a lot simpler than that. You come back because you're meant to."

"My life is pretty good right now," explained Carmen, reaching out to grasp Mark's hand with both of hers. "Herb is a good man and loves me. But if anything happens to you, I don't know what I'll do."

"I'll be fine," Mark assured her. "Our crew has been working really hard on what we have to do over there. Everyone in our company is a good Marine, trained and ready to go up against anyone or anything."

"Tell us about the guys in your unit."

"It starts with Captain Dylan. He's much older than the rest of us, maybe thirty, but totally experienced. Back in the Persian Gulf War he was doing what we're going to be doing. He's not going to let us put ourselves in harm's way. Then there's First Sergeant Ralston. He's really hard on us, but that's probably just the way Captain Dylan wants him to be. Better than anyone else they know if we screw up they'll probably be dead too. You've already met Angelo and I know he can be a real idiot sometimes, but he's still like my brother and I wouldn't want to go into war with anyone else. Then there's our buddy Larry. His real name is Hilario Valdespino but that was too long for Angelo to deal with. We're also tight with a Marine named Jimmy Sykes from Kansas. Angelo calls him Wichita."

"So what handle did Angelo give you?"

"Sis, I am known as Shark, which is pretty cool because they're killers and so are Marines."

Carmen held her head in her hands. "I don't want to think about you killing anyone."

Mark bit into his cheeseburger while watching Emmy pull a small package out of her purse.

"It's what we trained for. Better them than us."

"This is for you," said Emmy, handing him the package to unwrap.

"What's this, a book with nothing in it?" asked Mark. "How uh, cool is that?"

"It's called a journal, Mark. You can write down all your experiences in it."

"What, you mean like a diary?" he frowned.

"No, I mean like a journal."

"My Marines are going to think it's a diary."

"It'll be a way for you to let off some steam when you can't talk to us or anyone else," said Emmy. "You've always been a good writer."

"Not everyone will agree on that with you," laughed Mark. "It never seemed to help my grades."

"You should have just studied more," reminded his Mom. "More books and less girls and sports."

"Just put down thoughts, whatever they are," instructed Emmy. "The worst case scenario is you can always just throw it away when you're done with it."

"Like I'm really going to be able to throw away something you gave me?" he reminded her

*   *   *

The Executive Chef entered his office to find it already occupied.

"Hey Chef! I'll just be a second…"

"I hope."

Sous Chef Dudley was sitting at his boss's desk going through some invoices. He quickly got up for Dante to sit down.

"How's it going? Take Mark to the airport?"

Dante sat down in front of the computer.

"Yes I did."

"You two are more alike than you might think."

"What, you mean, like father and son?"

"No, I mean he might want to be a chef too."

"Mark, a chef? That would be news to me."

"I was blown away by it too!" admitted Dudley. "Mark was thinking he might want to be a chef but was afraid to tell you because you might say the best way for him to learn would be for him to work for you. That scared him even more than having to go over to Iraq."

"What the hell do you mean by that?"

"Well, you're a bit tough on those you love."

"Dudley, let's get this straight once and for all. I don't love you. In fact, I barely respect you."

"Chef, I'm really hurt by that," admitted Dudley, feigning some emotional pain. "Does this mean you're not picking up my contract next season?"

"Dudley, you don't have a contract. This is a right-to-work state. I think the most humane thing would be for you to just be eliminated. Do you really think I'm that tough to work for?"

"Well, some days are worse than others."

"Mark never mentioned any of this to me. Is this just a figment of your imagination brought on by all the crap smoked when you still had hair?"

"That's why I lost my hair?"

"Probably."

"Chef, he didn't say anything because of how he really sees you. He doesn't just see you as a father. He's seen how everyone here regards you like you're the General or something."

"A General? Why did he see me that way?"

"Well," thought Dudley, "maybe because of the correlation I might have helped make for him."

"What correlation would that be, Dudley?"

"It's just like the way you taught me," explained Dudley. "A kitchen is not a democracy but a chain of command. There has to be someone up at the top who sets the standards, creates the battle plan, then orders the Captains like me to go lead the troops into battle."

"I can't remember ever teaching you anything even remotely resembling that?"

"The great part is you don't have to!" exclaimed Dudley. "You lead by example, and it's really a great one. That's why we're the best well-oiled culinary army on the Strip. It's all you, man!"

Stephanie stuck her head in the doorway.

"How's it going, guys?"

"The Chef is really busting my chops today!" whined Dudley, hoping she would intercede. "I'm just a soldier trying to help fight the war."

"Stephanie, I really do need your help," pleaded Chef Dante. "You know more about hotel protocol than I do. Theoretically, I'm the General here, so can I court-martial Dudley, or just eliminate him right now?"

* * *

The bar down the road from the Marine base in San Diego was crowded as usual on a Friday night. Mark and his fellow Marines were having fun and Angelo's voice could be heard above the din, as usual.

Angelo eyed a sullen Hilarion Valdespino, who was silently drinking alone at the bar. "Hey Larry, who are you pulling for in the Super Bowl?"

The slightly built Cuban American didn't seem interested and obviously had other concerns on his mind. "I don't know or even care, man."

"Cheer the hell up, Larry!" suggested Angelo. "You been down in the dumps ever since we got here."

"Dude, my wife is now seven months pregnant and I'm going to be halfway around the world when my first son is born," explained Valdespino, shaking his head. "What if I don't come back and never even get a chance to know him? This is just not right!"

"Larry, that whole birthing process can be very messy," offered Angelo, consoling him with another beer. "Men don't really need to be around all that. Your wife is going to go crazy no matter if you're there or not. By the time you get back she won't be fat any more, that whole diaper thing will be under control, and there'll be lots of pictures of anything you missed. Trust me, you'll be better off with your fellow killers> This is where you belong."

Mark slapped Valdespino on the shoulder and laughed. "There, feeling better now?"

"Hey Wichita," called out Angelo down the bar, "who do you like in the game?"

"The Kansas City Chiefs," smiled the tall red-haired Marine with horn-rimmed glasses.

"The Chiefs aren't playing, dumb ass!"

"I'm talking next year," nodded Sykes.

A very grim First Sergeant Oliver Ralston appeared behind them to check on their collective condition, frowning at them all intently, as usual.

"First Sergeant!"

"Listen up! Captain Dylan will be due here any minute with his fiancée. You'd best not offend her!" warned Ralston, speaking directly at Angelo.

"We're cool, at least I am, First Sergeant," Lied Angelo. "It's these other guys I'm worried about."

Ralston looked them over, growled like a big lion, and ordered a drink to calm his nerves.

"I once saw a picture of Captain Dylan's girl," remarked Valdespino. "She's pretty hot."

"Captains get paid well enough to be able to afford hot women," said Mark.

"Like we can't?" argued Angelo, aghast. "Has the memory of our recent Vegas experience faded from your pea brain so quickly, my young Shark?"

"That was pretty special," Mark agreed with a smile. "What I remember of it, that is."

"You mean you guys scored some tail while you were in Vegas?" Even the remote possibility of it seemed to pull Valdespino out of his doldrums. "Please, I'm a married man, I need details...."

"All right," offered Angelo, leaning in as if he was dispensing some classified information, "check this out. Shark and I meet these two beauties on the plane to Vegas. We figured there must've been something wrong with them, like maybe they're dykes or something, because they really weren't buying into us the way most hot women in their right minds should do."

"That is," smiled Mark, "until they saw the limo driver waiting for us in baggage claim."

"You guys had a limousine?" asked Valdespino, becoming even more impressed by the minute.

"Shark's Dad hooked us up big time! It was sweet, at least twenty feet long with this no shit chauffeur in his little tux who had a sign with our names on it like we're some big freaking VIPs!"

"Everyone's eyes are on us, including the two babes who are waiting for a cab," interjected Mark. "Angelo just plays it off real casual like its standard operating procedure for us, and offers the girls a ride to their hotel in our limo."

"Did they go for it?"

"Oh, big time!" assured Angelo. "We hit town and in the first five minutes are hooked up with these two freaking gorgeous hot as hell blondes. I'll never forget them, Mary and Carol from Georgia."

"No, it was Carrie and Marilyn and they were from Chattanooga," corrected Mark.

"Whatever!" shrugged Angelo. "Those are not the kind of details Larry is looking for, Shark."

"What happened then?"

"Well Larry, we had to meet Shark's Dad and his family for dinner and a party in our honor and the girls had plans too, but later on we found them in the casino."

"They were already pretty wasted so we invited them up to our *suite* overlooking the Strip" continued Mark. "Things started getting hot and heavy and they almost split, but Angelo gave them that line about what happens in Vegas stays in Vegas, and how they were helping their country by supporting us Marines. Luckily, they were just drunk enough to buy into it. The rest of it was just like this surreal pornographic blur."

"Oh man!" Valdespino tried to visualize it, close to hyperventilating.

"Larry, not even your depraved imagination is fertile or twisted enough to begin considering the depths of debauchery we plunged into. I was still messed up when I got back to Chicago a few days later!" admitted a very grateful Angelo.

"Think they'll ever write to us, Angelo?"

"Who the hell cares?" shrugged Angelo, quickly snapping to attention. "Killers, Captain Dylan is in the house and yes, she is very hot!"

All the Marines stood up straight and saluted Captain Dylan as he sauntered over with a rather stunning fiancée on his arm. He returned their salute, then motioned for them to relax.

"Hoorah, Marines! This is my fiancee Caressa, who makes my life worthwhile enough to put up with y'all!" smiled the Captain in a Southern drawl. "Caressa Rose from San Francisco, meet First Sergeant Oliver Ralston from Pittsburgh, Lance Corporal Hilario Valdespino from Miami, Corporal James Sykes from Wichita, Private First Class Mark Sebastian from Las Vegas, and Private First Class Angelo Cicci from Chicago. These are but five of the fifty men in my company, but they're the Devil Dogs I keep closest."

Greetings were quickly exchanged all around. The Captain kissed his fiancee.

"I'll get us some drinks, honey."

Caressa looked at the men and they looked at her, followed by a briefly uncomfortable silence.

"Wait just a minute now," asked Angelo with a sneaking suspicion as he looked over her facial features carefully, "are you Italian?"

"Yes I am, about half of me actually," she replied. "You know what's funny, Angelo? Jeffrey told me all about you and predicted that would be the very first thing you would say to me."

"The Captain's got your number, Chee-Chee!" pointed out First Sergeant Ralston with a laugh.

"He is very predictable!" admitted Mark as all the others concurred.

"Yeah, I'm predictable all right. That's why none of these measly scoundrels here are even the least bit worried about me watching their backs over in Iraq," rebounded Angelo defiantly, finding his mates agreeing reluctantly. "I'm hair trigger predictable."

"Your Captain feels the same way," Caressa told them, "about all of you. He's been pushing you real hard but we all know what's at stake. I have my own selfish reasons since Jeffrey and I are going to be married this summer. I'd like him to be there for it."

"Will we be invited to the wedding?" ventured Sykes meekly, "I mean if we're still alive."

"No one invites you anywhere, Wichita,"

"You are all very welcome to come. My family would have never predicted I'd wind up marrying a Marine, but you'll all be part of our family now."

Captain Dylan returned with drinks and was not at all embarrassed to again kiss his girl in front of the men. They were duly impressed if not totally envious.

"Time for a toast," suggested Mark.

"Here's to the Marines!" toasted Caressa loudly before Angelo could even open his mouth. "It's always great to see a few good men."

"HOO-RAH!"

*   *   *

The phone rang past midnight in the chef's house. Dante quickly reached over to answer it.

"Dad, did I wake you?"

"No Mark, not to worry. Night owls like me are always awake," he yawned. "How are you doing?"

"We're leaving for Kuwait tonight, so this is probably going to be the last phone call you'll get from me for a while."

"Why didn't you let us know sooner?" asked a shocked Dante. "We could've come to see you off."

"They didn't tell us until this evening. I'm sorry. But don't worry, we're all pumped to go there and get our job done to get back home just as soon as we can."

"Mark, when you're a father you hope that a day like this will never come, but here it is... I don't know how to say what I'm really feeling right now."

"When I enlisted I didn't really consider how it would affect my whole family. Sorry about that. I promise I'll make it up to you all later. Did you see the Super Bowl? That's a good example of exactly the kind of butt-whipping performance we are going to put on Saddam and any team he lines up against us."

"I'm with you on that one hundred percent. If you have to fight, then protect yourself well but leave no doubt as to the outcome."

"It's kind of surreal, Dad. Just a few weeks ago I was free as a bird in Las Vegas, and a couple of weeks from now I'll probably be somewhere south of Baghdad going through who knows what.'"

"You've got my emails and my calling card in case you need it. Whatever you need, let us know and we'll get it to you soon as we can."

"Cool deal. Please keep an eye on Emmy, will you? The government says if we go to war there might be more terrorist attacks and you know how they like to target airplanes. She's flying all over the country and terrorists don't really care about anyone else since they plan on dying themselves anyway."

"Noted. Sometimes I wish I could somehow influence my children's decisions, but we raised you to have minds of your own. Both a blessing and a curse."

"It's better to have choices, don't you think? I mean, you could have chosen to be a Marine like Grandpa and Uncle Ray, and gone into the family beer distribution business too. But you chose to do neither and became a chef people admire. I really respect that."

"Thank you, son. You'll have your own choices to make when you get back."

"What do you mean by that?"

"Well, Dudley told me about a conversation you may have had with him."

"That weasel! He promised not to say anything"

"You know Dudley. He's imperfect and tortured. Torn between loyalty and friendship, the weight of a simple secret threatened to sink him."

"Don't be too hard on Dudley, Dad. He really does look up to you."

"He looks up to me as an example? Like you look up to your Captain or a General?"

"Exactly! Dad, there's one other thing. I know you and Mom don't exactly see eye to eye anymore, maybe never really did. But you guys and Emmy are all I have, so could you call her once in a while and maybe exchange information about me or anything else."

"Sure, I can do that."

"I know you can, but will you?"

"I'll make it a point. Did you call her tonight?"

"Not home. She thought I left next week."

"Don't worry, I'll call and take care of it. I'll tell her how much you love and miss her."

"Thanks. By the way, I really like Stephanie, Dad. I'm happy that you're happy with her. I don't know if you realize this, but you've really sort of mellowed out a lot since you met her."

"Thank you, Mark. I'm glad I've mellowed out even though I'm probably the last to know I even needed to. Is Dudley behind this too?"

"No, I don't think he's even caught on to the whole Stephanie thing yet."

"Good, I feel a lot better then."

"Dad, I love you."

"I love you too, son," Dante spoke softly as his voice was beginning to break.

"Don't worry, Dad. I'll be alive and well in Las Vegas next New Year's Eve. That's a promise," said Mark with an assured voice. "I'm a Marine, and I only lie when I'm playing cards!"

February 2003

In a tent on another hot and sweaty night, Mark began writing a letter while swatting away flies and picking fleas off his arms.

Dear Dad,

We've been in Kuwait since last Friday. The mail takes a few weeks to get back home, so by the time you read this hopefully the phones will be working and I'll have called by then.

It was a pretty rough flight over. Since it was a military transport and we were packing all our gear it got pretty cramped inside. We were side by side on benches with our legs wedged between the row of Marines facing right across from us. This was for about twenty four hours straight in the air. If you had to relieve yourself you had to use the rope and pulley on the ceiling to pass over the top of everyone else just to get to the hole. Believe me, I'll never complain to Emmy about having to sit in an economy coach seat ever again.

We arrived at the Kuwait City airport sometime after midnight and they immediately packed us into a bus for a ride about an hour away to our new home at Camp Commando. I guess it's okay to tell you where we are. There are about fifty thousand Marines out here in tents, so I'm sure the Iraqis already know where we are since the border is only about two hours away.

Camp Commando (or *Cammando* as we Marines call it) is a pretty amazing place when you consider the logistics of creating a huge tent city and headquarters out in the middle of the desert in about six weeks. They've trucked in mobile kitchens, showers, toilets, a gym, satellite dishes, and the phone trailer should be up soon.

The food is actually fairly decent here and there's a lot of it. I'm sure we won't be eating as well once we get the call to go into Iraq, so we're making the most of a good thing now.

The weather here is absolutely brutal. At least a hundred degrees outside every day and the sandstorms blow in at forty miles an hour. The sand is really fine powder, almost like flour. It gets in your nose and ears and eyes, as well as any other exposed openings in your body. It's all over our gear, our weapons, and uniforms.

We don't have any choice but to make the best of it. We wear goggles and scarves when we're out on maneuvers in the desert. Then there are the flies and fleas, huge swarms of them everywhere just feeding and breeding on us. There are also lots of wild dogs roaming outside the base. Some guys want to adopt them but our officers won't allow it.

Since we're expecting the Iraqis to probably use biological weapons on us by way of a missile attack, we have drills almost every day and have to carry around our weapons and chemical gear at all times. When the raid siren sounds we get into our chemical suits, put on our gas masks, and then pile into one of the Scud bunkers at the camp. Sometimes we have to stay there for an hour or more until we get the all-clear signal.

Should we ever start to feel the effects of nerve gas we have Atropine and some chloride compounds. We're supposed to jam big needles into our thighs if we feel anything bad happening. Definitely not fun stuff, but we have to deal with it now so the rest of the world doesn't have to later.

The rest of the time we go on maneuvers, fill sandbags, clean and re-clean our weapons, play cards, and discuss getting the job done quickly so we can all go home. Everyone's pretty positive about doing whatever we have to do to get it done.

It's fairly safe here since we have multiple rows of barbed wire, fences and blast walls around the camp perimeter. We have a big weapons range about ten miles from the border and the 50 caliber machine gun that I man on top of the Captain's Humvee is responding very well to my touch. I really hope I don't have to use it too much, but if anyone gives me cause then may God have mercy on them because neither I nor my weapon will.

Feel free to pass this letter around to the rest of the family if you want. I don't know when I'll have time to write to everyone, but I'll try. Some guys who have been here for a while say it takes at least two weeks to get any care packages from home if anyone cares to take the hint. Just tell everyone I'm fine and that I'm thinking about them all the time. I hope to see you all real soon.

Love, Mark

*   *   *

The Marine base in Northern Kuwait was nearly dark and mostly quiet as the oppressively hot night blew swirling sand over, around, and through the tents with a whistling roar the base had already become quite used to.

"You know what I think we should do when we get back home?" suggested Angelo as they grouped themselves over a makeshift table playing cards under a dim light. The four Marines were sweating through their undershirts as if they had showered in them. Valdespino was tapping the table with a Latin rhythm and Sykes was scratching himself.

"What you should do is to figure out that no one really cares about what you think," Mark informed him, generating chuckles from the Marines.

"We've been trying to tell you that for a very long time," seconded Valdespino.

"Screw you guys," replied Angelo. "Seriously, when we get back home we should pool our resources together and open up a cool club somewhere, maybe in Las Vegas. Mark's Uncle Ray can get us all the booze, Mark's Dad can handle the food part, Wichita will be our Midwest prime beef connection, and Larry's people know the hospitality end of it so the way I see it we've already got all the bases covered."

"My *people* don't really know the hospitality business," Valdespino corrected him. "My father-in-law just works at a hotel as a bellman."

"So how do you fit into the picture, Angelo?" Sykes wanted to know, somewhat skeptical.

"Me? Well, I'm the guy with the vision," related Angelo with all due humility. "I know how clubs should look and how they should be run. I know all the best Deejays and what it takes to lure in all the hottest babes. Most importantly, my family is very successful and I'm sure they'd be willing to invest in a profitable venture if I play my cards right. As your dwindling finances have sadly discovered, I always play my cards right."

"Wait a minute, isn't your family in the funeral home business?" checked Mark, more than a little bit confused. "Why would they set you up in a nightclub?"

"Because when I come home a freaking war hero, in appreciation of the sacrifice for my country, and with the clear understanding that once I readjust to society I will someday join the family business like my father wants me to, he will float the money for a club."

"Have you advised him of your intentions yet?" inquired Sykes, a bit sarcastically.

"No Wichita, but that time will soon come. I'm a spoiled rich kid from Chicago. I will get my way, just like I always do," Angelo assured them confidently. "All my older brothers will be on my side too. Believe me, there's already enough internal arguing about how to run the business that they'll be more than happy to do whatever they can to keep my big mouth out of the way for as long as they possibly can."

"You'll have to count me out," advised Sykes, shaking his head, feigning disappointment. "I've got a farm to take care of and Becky wants to try and get pregnant the same day I get home."

"Afraid I'm out too," nodded Valdespino sadly. "All I want to do is get back to Miami with my wife and son, and go back to selling cars. I'm really good at it and can hook you dudes up with a good deal."

"I guess it's up to you and me then, Shark," said Angelo, shaking his head disappointedly at the poor choices his fellow Marines were making.

First Sergeant Ralston stormed into the tent with a typically angry scowl on his face, looking around for something to chew on. He spied the weapons besides their cots and went over to inspect.

"Don't mind me, ass wipes, but I don't have anything better to do than check up on your worthless butts. *Chee-Chee*, what the hell is this?"

"That is an M-16 rifle, First Sergeant."

"I know what the hell it is! Are you or are you not the Captain's driver?"

"Yes, I certainly am, First Sergeant," replied Angelo proudly, "and if I may say so myself I am the best damn driver in the whole company."

"Don't lie to me, *Chee-Chee*! Don't make that mistake!" warned Ralston as his voice rose and he loomed over Angelo menacingly while holding the M-16 with a look of disgust. "The Captain only carries a pistol when riding in his Humvee, is that not right?"

"That's correct, First Sergeant," said Angelo, unsure of exactly what he'd done to receive First Sergeant Ralston's quickly escalating wrath.

"Are you not going to give him your rifle if he needs to blow the shit out of some crazy Iraqis? Of course you will," screamed Ralston, "so why in the hell would you give him this filthy rifle that is going to no shit jam up the first damn time he tries to fire it? Are you trying to get the Captain killed?"

"I just cleaned it yesterday!"

"Y*e-ye-yesterday*?" Ralston's eyes opened even wider, absolutely incredulous at how wrong the answer was. "Yesterday is dead and gone! It no longer exists. This is today's dirt! Now I repeat, are you trying to get your Captain killed, Private First Class?"

"No! All right, I'll clean it!" Angelo, hurryied to get up from the card game.

First Sergeant Ralston thrust the weapon roughly into Angelo's arms and went looking for another weapon to critically inspect. "Lance Corporal Valdespino, is this your weapon?"

"Yes, First Sergeant!"

"This is very, very nice, Corporal," observed First Sergeant Ralston with continuous nods of approval. "So as you can see, *Chee-Chee*, Corporal Valdespino is my driver and he in fact is the best driver in this company because should I have to ever reach over and use his weapon to bring my wrath down upon the enemy I can sure as hell *guar-an-damn-tee* you this weapon will be in a pristine operating condition for me to render my profane justice with!"

"Larry's very anal about keeping his weapon clean, like it's his ass. I'll try to be more like him."

"Yes, see that you do!" suggested First Sergeant Ralston in the strongest possible terms as he left the tent while still snarling.

"I told you to clean it man," Mark reminded a fuming Angelo as he began disassembling his rifle. "You're just too damn stubborn to be smart."

"Shut the hell up, Shark!" pleaded Angelo. "You guys know what? I think the First Sergeant is really starting to turn into a *fun sponge...*"

* * *

Stephanie accompanied Chef Dante as he hurried through the very busy back kitchen to check on the progress of several projects.

"Heard anything from Mark?" she asked.

"He called today from a base in Kuwait."

"How did he sound?"

"Pretty good. He can't tell me much about what is going on, but it sounds like he's handling it well."

"So how are you holding up?" she asked, placing a gentle hand on his arm.

"I keep busy and positive and try not to worry," confessed Dante. "But all I read and hear leads me to believe we are going to war come hell or high water. A lot of fine young men are going to be forced to give up their lives and if my son happens to be one of them then the world is going to have one hell of an angry man to deal with. Other than that, I'm in love with this wonderful woman who entered my life when I least expected it, and I'm trying hard not to let everything else going on in my life affect my relationship with her. So I guess I'm doing fine…"

He gave Stephanie a gentle squeeze on the hand, and got a warm smile from her as they separated to head down opposite corridors.

"See you later…" he promised.

"I'll wait up. Try not to be too late."

*   *   *

The brutal wind and heat died down after night fell, leaving Angelo and Mark sitting outside looking up at the stars smoking cheap cigars and swatting away flies. Angelo suddenly smiled.

"You know what? It's Valentine's Day!"

"Is it?"

"Did I tell you about my girl back home?"

"No, but you've told me about all the girls you've *had* back home."

"I mean the one I'll marry when I get back."

"Right, Angelo…"

"I'm serious, man." Angelo leaned over, giving every credible indication he actually meant what he was saying. "Look, I've played fast and loose with the neighborhood babes all my life but this girl, she's not like them. She's the kind of girl you marry, not just screw around with. Here, let me show you her picture."

Angelo quickly produced a small snapshot and handed it over proudly.

"She's cute, very cute. What's her name?"

"Teresa, but everyone calls her Terri."

"Isn't she a little young, even for you?"

"Not really. I'm almost twenty one and she's like sixteen or seventeen, but she'll be graduating high school next year so it'll all work out fine."

"Sixteen?" laughed Mark. "What are you, a cradle robber? Have you even asked her yet?"

"Just a formality," assured Angelo. "I've known her my whole life. We grew up on the same street. She was always like this little sister to me but as soon as she started to develop, she's had this mad crush on me ever since. She won't even date other guys. My mother had a dream that I was going to marry her someday. Once she made the mistake of telling Terri about it, the jig was pretty much up. It will make our families very happy."

"Well, I am definitely surprised and somewhat impressed, Angelo. Contrary to popular opinion, you just might have a heart after all?"

"Don't you tell anyone!" Angelo admonished, taking the picture back. "I have a certain image I have to keep up around here so you and the other guys won't start wetting your pants once the shooting starts."

"Thank God for that, and lucky us having you to protect us all!" replied Mark, breathing a sigh of relief. "So tell me more about her…"

"All right!" agreed Angelo, leaning in closer to divulge juicy details. "There was this one night, it was her birthday, and I gave her this bracelet I picked up from a guy downtown. Maybe it was stolen, but the price was right. Anyway, no one had ever given her a big girl's bracelet before. So after the party…"

* * *

Captain Dylan carefully looked out over the command tent filled with the fifty eager men under his command. The tent flaps were closed as the wind howled and blasted sand outside.

"Most of you know a lot of units have started for the border and we should be joining them soon."

Cheers filled the tent.

"This is war and we don't expect a walk in the park, but we do expect to have air superiority, more firepower, a better battle plan, and much better fighters than the enemy. Even if they choose to use chemical weapons it will only slow us down a bit. Be assured we will win, and decisively. I know most of you would rather be out there in the thick of the battle with the forward units rather than being part of a Force Service Support Group like we are, but the job we do is still a very important asset to this division. Listen up! Who is ready to go and kick some Iraqi ass?"

Cheers erupted again, growing in volume.

"That's what I thought. Our job is not going to be easy and that's why they have us doing it. We've had all of the training we need. We are the world's finest, most deadly fighting force. If they want to use chemical weapons on us, that's just one more reason to mess them up even more. Still, you sure as hell better wear your MOPP and have your gas mask with you at all times. Also make sure you're wearing your flak and helmet unless we tell you otherwise. They gave us this gear for a reason and we will use it."

Captain Dylan paced before the Marines, making eye contact with as many as he could.

"Every one of you will have your weapon on you at all times and be ready to use it. Before we mount the vehicles, you will obey the command to go to Condition One. Once over the border, any Iraqi with a weapon is fair game but remember the Rule of

Engagement. We will not be shooting a bunch of women and children. Good to go?"

The loud answer was affirmative.

"The most important thing to remember is that we are Marines. Every Marine is a Rifleman and the most deadly instrument on the face of the Earth is a Marine with an M-16. We are going to be supporting a unit called Mortuary Affairs. A lot of you may not know what that is, but Mortuary Affairs makes sure no Marine ever gets left behind on the battlefield. We can only hope they won't have too much work to do."

More cheers filled the tent.

"Be smart and stay alert. Remember all of your training and follow your Squad Leaders. The Iraqis and their terrorist friends threw down the gauntlet with 9/11. Now it's pay back time and they are going to wish they never screwed with the United States of America! Are there any questions? Good. Now get your gear on. Squad Leaders, Comm checks in 15 mikes. SP 0530."

"HOO-RAH!" The tent shook as all the Marines answered with a roar.

"If I was a freaking Iraqi and knew this bunch of killers was mounting up to go across the breach after me, I'd be shitting my pants and jumping on my camel to get the hell out of Dodge," advised Angelo while hurrying out of the tent with the others. "These sorry shits are about to find out how futile it is to engage in combat with the United States Marines."

"Amen!" agreed all his fellow Marines.

*   *   *

Stephanie Lawrence sat on the couch in her condo, petting the beautiful white cat draped across her lap. She checked the time and turned on the television. A female commentator immediately filled the screen.

"Hello, this is Diana Scott and welcome again to 'Three Voices' where each and every week we discuss news of the world with a trio of guests with often dissimilar views. The focus of our program tonight will be the impending war with Iraq. Joining me today are three men we always enjoy having on the show. First, Democratic Congressman Wayne Ballantree. Always a pleasure to have you back."

"Thank you, Diana," smiled the Representative.

"Next up is a familiar face who will become this network's lead war analyst should we invade Iraq, retired Army General Fitzpatrick Pynchon."

"Nice to be here with you, Diana," voiced the crew cut, graying soldier.

"Finally, we are pleased to have one of the most respected commentators in the world of Arab journalism, our good friend Kassim Al Khayyam."

"*Shoukran,* Miss Scott, you are very kind," said the Arab journalist.

"All right gentlemen," began Diana Scott. "Let's focus on the situation in Iraq. Every day the rhetoric for going to war is rising. The President is warning that our nation's safety depends on ending this direct and growing threat to us. He is also declaring we will lead in carrying out the urgent and dangerous work of destroying chemical and biological weapons. But there still remains some doubt that solid evidence justifying the need to go to war with Iraq exists."

"It's there!" advised General Pynchon.

"Recently," continued Diana Scott, "British spy novelist John Le Carre wrote 'How Bush and his junta succeeded in deflecting America's anger for Osama bin Laden towards Saddam Hussein is one of the great public relations conjuring tricks in history'. Have we gone too far to turn back now, or is there any way we can still avert going to war in Iraq? General Pynchon?"

"John Le Carre? He writes fiction, doesn't he? Enough said about that. Saddam Hussein has not complied with any of the United Nations resolutions to allow inspections of his weapons of mass destruction facilities. That's a clear indication he has something to hide. We can't wait while some of those materials are smuggled out of the country or wind up in the hands of terrorists like the Al Qaeda network. We don't have any alternative but to go in and clean the place up."

"I also believe we have passed the point of no return, Diana," offered Congressman Ballantree, "but I haven't supported the way in which we've been going about this process from the very beginning. Congress authorized the President to enforce the UN resolutions. But most lawmakers felt it would be with the tacit approval of the UN for any enforcement. But this Administration could care less what the United Nations or the rest of the world approves of. We have a cowboy riding with cavalry looking everywhere for Indians."

"Oh come on now, Wayne," protested General Pynchon, "you know as well as I do the UN couldn't find a piece of crap in a manure pile."

"If I'd seen firm evidence that any or all of these supposed dangers to America really existed," continued Ballantree, "I might've supported the President. But all I've seen are spurious intelligence reports, second hand information, very questionable data, and an extremely conservative point of view on how to proceed. Quite frankly, none of this looks very good for either America or the rest of the world."

"We have good sound intelligence that they are harboring dangerous weapons of mass destruction!"

glared General Pynchon. "I for one do not want to see 9/11 all over again with chemical toxins and nuclear weapons in the mix! Maybe you're willing to take that chance, but I sure as hell won't! Proof after the fact, after another major terrorist attack, is not the proof America is really looking for."

"In the absence of hard evidence, suspicion plus assumption plus exaggeration still does not equate to the truth no matter how loudly you trumpet it," argued Congressman Ballantree. "I'm actually hearing very little positive support from my constituents for what now seems inevitable. We have a lot of military bases in my state and families are being deeply affected."

"Will escalating protests against the impending war have any effect on this administration's actions?" Diana Scott asked him.

"A lot of Americans are protesting against this war, and what every patriotic American needs to realize is just because someone protests against the decision to go to war it doesn't mean the protesters won't support our troops there, or are in any way less patriotic. Many of these protests are from military families who have loved ones going to Iraq. But this administration is making it seem like all protesters are anti-American and somehow helping promote terrorism because they don't agree with the invasion plans. This is an extremely knee-jerk, ludicrous position for the executive branch of our government to take. This administration's policies continue to reflect the epitome of hypocrisy."

"Spoken like a true Democrat."

"Maybe we'll find out this war really was necessary and the White House did exactly the right thing in eliminating an immediate threat to our country," continued Ballantree, ignoring the General's comments. "I truly hope so because otherwise there will be hell to pay in trying to explain to the families of those who will die or be maimed for life exactly why the sacrifice their loved ones had to make was really necessary if the reason for going to war in the first place was all just a great big lie. I am certainly not the only person in this country who is concerned about where this country is being led, or rather *misled*."

"Thank you, Congressman," nodded Diana Scott. "Mr. Al Khayyam, what is your opinion?"

"I believe you have a very wily President who barely won an election under somewhat questionable circumstances," began Al Khayyam's succinct analysis. "He mostly floundered on the job until he received an unprecedented surge of popularity due to 9/11. Why, because three thousand Americans died in this tragedy? Because he vowed to find out who was responsible and punish them? What leader would not do the same? But the polls rise, so his advisers decide it best to portray him a wartime President and quickly tie 9/11 to Iraq."

"Preposterous!" thundered the General.

"Yes, precisely, isn't it?" smiled Al Khayyam. "In my humble opinion, the decision by the White House to go to war was actually made a long time ago. I believe hawkish advisers made plans to go after Saddam Hussein during the first months of his administration, well before the attacks on the World Trade Center. When you activate hundreds of thousands of troops and start shipping huge quantities of supplies to the Persian Gulf it is no longer a bluff or an exercise. You are, how you say here, good to go."

"Thank you, Sir."

"But that is not all, Miss Scott," continued the journalist. "Add to this the premature announcement in early January that massive reconstruction contracts had already been awarded to repair everything the United

States was planning to level in Iraq, all of which would presumably be paid for by Iraqi oil, and the picture becomes clear. These contracts were awarded to some of the administration's biggest campaign contributors."

"That's not how it all came down!" claimed the General, pointing an accusing finger.

"While all this is happening, the White House is repeating *'Al Qaeda, 9/11, Saddam Hussein, Weapons of Mass Destruction'* over and over again as if it were a mantra," explained the Arab journalist with a touch of sarcasm. "When they say it enough it almost sounds like it is all connected. This war is in fact a business and political proposition promoted under a veil of fear and retribution the White House, and not any terrorists, are holding over the people of America. What this war is all about, and if you say it enough times and string it together you will see what I mean. *Oil, oil, oil, oil,...*"

"For Christ's sake, Khayyam, give us a break, will you?" pleaded the General. "I have never heard such a jumble of poppycock before in my entire life!"

"We'll be back with more of 'Three Voices' after this message," promised Diana Scott.

March 2003

The Marines were sitting outside their tent going through gear in the late afternoon sun.

"Angelo, you've given us all nicknames but you don't have one yourself?" questioned Sykes.

"Yeah *Angie*, why is that?" teased Mark.

"What the hell did you just call me?"

"*Angie*. Isn't that always the default nickname for Angelo? I'm sure your family must've given you a handle when you were growing up? Was it *Angie*?"

"Screw you, Shark! Just quit with your endless stream of shit! When I was growing up my nickname was *Piccolo Diavolo,* meaning 'Little Devil' to all you poor fools who don't know Italian. I used to raise hell but everyone still loved me. You want to call me something? Call me *The Devil* because I plan on dispatching a whole lot of Iraqis straight to hell!"

"Now, you plan on doing this while driving a Humvee?" ventured Valdespino, examining the logistics of it all. "How, by running people over or something?"

"If I have to, I will!" nodded Angelo. "Besides, the Captain said Shark and I can trade-off between driving and blasting shit sometimes."

"He didn't say anything about that to me.".

"Well don't be holding your breath waiting for Captain Dylan to run shit by you for your approval."

"Even though this war is real, somehow I think it's almost going to be like a movie," mused Valdespino, beating fingers on his rifle.

"My all-time favorite war movie is *Apocalypse Now*," related Angelo. "I just saw the Director's cut a few months ago and they put in this cool scene where Charlie Sheen's hard-ass dad goes to this wicked

French plantation where he gets shit-faced stoned and then laid by this pale-skinned Frog nympho."

"The movie I really liked was *Full Metal Jacket,* offered Sykes. "That was the bomb!"

"*Platoon* was wicked," offered Valdespino. "and that Mel Gibson movie was pretty good too."

"*We Were Soldiers*?" asked Sykes.

"Guys, did you ever read the book it was based on?" questioned Angelo, shaking his head ruefully. "No, I didn't think so. If you'd read the book you wouldn't have liked the movie as much. It didn't even tell half the freaking story and they completely forgot to mention the column of soldiers who left that fight and were cut to ribbons in a gook ambush a few days later."

"It was just one of those typical Hollywood rim jobs where the bosses don't think the real story is good enough so they make up some new crap to make their stars look better," agreed Mark. "For example, the Colonel Moore character Mel played? In the book a lot of the heroic stuff was actually done by this ass-kicking Englishman named Rick Rescorla, who died on 9/11 during the attack at the World Trade Center."

"You're far more observant than I thought."

"Thanks, but it's my Dad who is really more observant, Angelo. I actually liked the movie and then he made me read the book and it ruined the experience for me. I hate it when he does that."

"Think they'll make movies about this war?"

"They make movies about every war, Larry, it's what they do." Angelo assured him. "Filmmakers like to blow shit up and filmgoers love to see it. Maybe they'll make one about what we wind up doing here?"

"Yeah, right!" nodded Sykes skeptically.

"You really think so?" wondered Larry.

"I think we should all seriously start considering who should play our parts in a movie, since it will be our freaking story to sell," suggested Angelo.

"All right," agreed Mark. "I'll have my agent call yours and see if we can work this thing out."

"Say, why don't we all do lunch?" asked Valdespino, tired of baking in the sun.

The four Marines took him up on the suggestion, stashing their gear in the tent and then sauntering off toward the mess hall, still in serious negotiations about their impending movie careers.

"For me," offered Angelo, "the obvious choice would be…"

* * *

Chef Dante was working on production menus in his office when the phone rang.

"Hello, this is Chef Sebastian…"

"Hey Dad!" called out a sweaty Mark.

"Mark! My God, so good to hear from you!"

"Right back at you. I just wanted to call and thank the hotel for sending us the care package. It was massive. Must've cost a lot just to ship it."

"Our hotel remembers VIPs. I'm not quite sure what they sent. It's been really busy around here and Stephanie took care of all the details."

"Thank her for us. I had a lot to share with my Marines. I was having stomach problems that morning and was in the latrine when the mail was delivered. Angelo totally pissed me off because he couldn't even wait until I got back to open the box. Even though it was addressed to me, he figured it was for him too."

"I'm glad you enjoyed it. Feeling better?"

"Back to normal. Probably eating too much dust. We're getting ready to move forward, but there's no way the Iraqis can stop us."

"The end game is not in doubt. The only variables are who gets hurt in the process. Let's get this over with quickly so you can get back home."

"Sounds like a good plan. Listen, there are a lot of Marines waiting in line to use the phone so if I don't get a chance to call Emmy, tell her I got her letter and really appreciate her thoughts. Gotta go now, love you."

"Love you too Mark, and I'm proud of you."

As soon as he hung up the phone, the door opened and a sheepish Sous Chef Dudley sautered in wearing a soiled apron.

"Hey, Chef. You wanted to see me?"

"Yes. Thank you so much for taking the time out from your busy schedule."

"No problem. I'm sorry about how that last luncheon went, and that whole health inspection thing didn't really come out the way I expected it to."

"It's not a problem we can't fix. It was just poor planning and wishful thinking. Hey, maybe you should be working in Washington?"

"Washington? Are you going to fire me?"

"Do I have a reason to?"

"I don't know, maybe?"

"Mark being sent to Iraq has made me a little crazy, but not that crazy. If anything happens to my son I'm not going to be able to keep this operation running smoothly. I won't even care any more. You need to be able to take over in such a contingency, so I am promoting you to Assistant Executive Chef."

"You're screwing with me!"

"Not this time. You've put up with a lot of crap and long hours here but I look first to you when I really need someone I can depend on, and everyone in this hotel knows that. I've made the mistake before of not telling the people how important they are, but I won't make that mistake again. I hope you know when I put you down it's only to help strengthen your humility."

"Wow, I'm now the Assistant EC!" grinned Dudley, barely able to believe his good fortune.

"Congratulations!" smiled Dante.

"When you were putting me through hell you were just trying to make me better?"

"Actually in the beginning I was trying to get rid of you. But now I might really need you."

"So, does this mean if Mark doesn't come back I don't get to keep the job?"

"No, the job is yours to lose. You deserve it, and my son will be coming home."

* * *

Two hours later the missile hit the camp without any warning. There was the sound of something coming in very fast, but there was no warning from the camp intercom system. The missile struck hard with a tremendous explosion that shook the ground violently.

Marines ran from their tents struggling to get on their chemical gear. They flew into the bunkers in a mad crush, everyone breathing hard and waiting for the next explosion to hit. Twenty minutes later, the all-clear signal sounded and cautious Marines returned into the glaring sunlight to assess the damage. A fifty foot crater was smoking in the middle of the camp.

"Where the hell was *The Big Loud Voice* over the speakers?" asked Angelo, pulling off his mask and hurried toward the tent with Mark, Larry, and Sykes.

"Don't know, dude, but this shit isn't right!"

They hurried into their tent, clearly shook up from the experience. The Marines peeled off the rest of their gear but kept it close by, not knowing what to expect next. First Sergeant Ralston stormed into the tent, still wearing his chemical suit.

"All my killers okay? Good to go?"

"Good to go!" repeated one after the other.

"Then get ready to mount up and kick some ass! Higher just informed us we're stepping off for the LD as soon as the sun sets. This is not a drill. That's right, Devil Dogs, we're heading for the Line of Departure, the Iraqi border. Move it! Comm checks in 15 mikes!"

The Marines jumped up to get their gear in order, adrenaline pumping. After six weeks of waiting they'd finally got the word they'd been waiting to hear. Mark smiled as he saw the determination in their eyes.

*   *   *

Chef Dante sat in his family room watching tv.

Commentators were announcing a Decapitation Attack aimed at Saddam Hussein and other Iraqi leaders had been launched. The war began with forty cruise missiles and F-117 Stealth Fighters hitting Baghdad. Elements of the Third Army Division and Mark's own 1st Marine Expeditionary Force were pouring over the Iraq border from Kuwait in a twenty-mile long convoy of steel destruction. The British were securing Basra and the Al Faw peninsula. Residents were fleeing Baghdad as the shock and awe campaign commenced.

A determined President was speaking on tv.

"American and coalition forces are in the early stages of military operations to disarm Iraq, free its people, and defend the world from grave danger. This will not be a campaign of half measures. We accept no outcome except victory. We will pass through this time of peril and carry on the work of peace. We will defend our freedom and bring freedom to others. We shall prevail. God bless America and those who defend her."

Dante switched channels and the dejected face of a Senator illed the screen.

"Today, I weep for my country," the Senator began sadly. "No more is the image of America one of a strong yet benevolent peacekeeper. Around the globe, our friends mistrust us, our word is disputed, and our intentions questioned. We flaunt our superpower status with arrogance. After the war has ended the United States will have to rebuild much more than Iraq. We have to rebuild America's image around the globe."

* * *

MARK'S JOURNAL:

I really didn't think I was ever going to write in this book, but now I figure it might be a good way to remember everything when I get home and everyone wants to know what really happened over here. The war has definitely started, but not in the way we expected it to. We were up all night working, caught a few hours sleep, and now we're getting ready to move out. Where are we? Still in Kuwait, but we hope to cross the LD later on today. So here's what happened:

We left Cammando the night before last and immediately got stuck in a big traffic jam heading for the Iraqi border. There were more tanks than I've ever seen before, plus armored personnel carriers, trucks, and Humvees all headed in the same direction. Until the traffic started moving over the LD you sat in your vehicle and just waited your turn to move up.

We watched the artillery show all night. Jets and artillery pounding Southern Iraq like we'd never seen anywhere before, so I can only imagine what Baghdad was getting hit with. The campaign was very impressive from where we were watching, and that's why it's surprising anyone is foolish enough to take on the full might of the American military. Everyone on the highway, Marines and Army, were pumped and ready to go, just waiting to lend their hand to the war.

It was also a little scary too. What if ground forces the size of ours were lined up to cross into the United States? We'd pound the holy shit out of them right where they sat, but the Iraqis don't have much of an air force compared to ours. They do have tanks and artillery and missiles. They must know where we are since a missile hit inside Cammando before we left, and we know they have chemical weapons so everyone has to be alert since we don't really know what is going to happen. Yesterday by mid-afternoon the convoy started to move ahead slowly, meaning we were good to go.

The bombing continued up ahead and the main convoy extended both as far in front of me as I could see, and as far behind me as I could see from my post in the machine gun turret on the Humvee. A Marine's ability to fight better than anyone else is partly due to our ability to communicate well, and Captain Dylan's radio always seemed to be broadcasting something.

I really couldn't hear much from where I was, but Angelo told me later it sounded like a lot of heavy shit was going down ahead of us. Not that Angelo would know many details. He's not very good with technical codes and military jargon. Maybe it's one of the reasons why Captain Dylan puts up with him.

Then, all of the sudden in just a matter of seconds, everything quickly changed as something serious had obviously happened. Higher command was on the phone to the Captain, and he relayed messages back to the First Sergeant and the rest of our company's convoy. Angelo pulled the Humvee off the highway onto the desert. Larry followed in his Humvee, then our AAV and two trucks fell in behind. Coming up the desert behind them in all the dust being created was another unit and I knew it had to be Mortuary Affairs since those are the people we support. Marines must have already died somewhere or they sure as hell wouldn't be calling for Mortuary Affairs.

It started to get dark and the Captain ordered our convoy to hold up just off the highway while he brought up all the platoon leaders, the First Sergeant, the Lieutenant, and they huddled for a moment with some Mortuary Affairs officers who ran up. Then everyone hurried back to their vehicles and we headed off to the northeast, away from the main convoy.

We didn't know at first what the hell was going on but the Captain explained it to us quickly, just as he'd instructed the other officers to do with their men. A CH-46 Sea Knight helicopter had gone down in northeastern Kuwait near the Al Faw peninsula. The first rescue units on the scene reported there were no survivors among the U.S. and British Marines on board. No reason was given for the crash, so we didn't know if it was because of hostile fire or not.

Our job was to escort Mortuary Affairs across the desert to the scene so they could arrange for any remains to be sent home. Two platoons of Marines would be alone all the way, with air and artillery support if we encountered any resistance. The Captain told us there was a good possibility we could engage some Iraqis along the way and to remember the rule of engagement and to exercise good trigger discipline.

If our convoy got hit we would call Higher Command immediately and evacuate the casualty to the Company Gunny. If one of us got hit we were to stay calm and take cover. The Medic would be right there with us. He told us to remember all the things we had talked about and all the training we'd done. The enemy was not a match for us and if proof was necessary to convince them, they would all die in the process.

Ten vehicles headed across the desert away from everyone else. Angelo was instructed to keep going until he hit a dirt road and then to proceed due East. It was a better ride from there but still bumpy and really dusty since darkness brought a sandstorm with it. I was in the lead vehicle so the dust wasn't as bad for me as it would be for those following behind us.

The lights of the main convoy soon started to fade away to the west. We could see and hear the constant bombardment from across the border as we quickly distanced ourselves from everyone else and were soon traveling alone across a very dark desert with our visibility severely hampered by all the sand hitting us. I wish I could've crawled down into the back but we were in the lead vehicle and if we saw any enemy, mine would be the first Marine weapon warning the others.

We drove on for hours, barely able to see. I don't think I've ever felt that tense before, but I'm sure it's probably just going to get worse from here. We were ready for anything to happen, but nothing did. I didn't have to fire a shot. The Captain was in constant communication and never seemed worried. Angelo did well under the conditions and almost ran us off the road only once. We started to see lights and hear activity up ahead and finally reached our destination.

Some Marines had already come in on copters and there were some British too. The crash debris was strewn over a good-sized area and it was easy to see no one could have possibly survived the explosion. There wasn't much left of the bodies from what I could tell.

During training some older Marines told us you get used to the sight of dead bodies when you see enough of them, but I don't know if I'll ever believe that to be true. Being attached to MA there's a distinct possibility we will be exposed to a lot of dead Marines, but if the war goes well we can hope there isn't much for us to see in that regard.

As we were protecting Mortuary Affairs we set up a wide perimeter around the crash site and took over from the advance units who were there. A few teams were dispatched to search around for more scattered debris in the surrounding area. In order to do that, we had to set up portable lights. There was a risk in lighting up the area so much that it drew attention from the enemy, but the crash site and all its evidence also had to be secured. If the enemy was out there, they'd be coming at us hard no matter what we did anyway.

Now the sun is up and the sand has died down. We've done about all we can do here and our MA and the Brits MA have made the necessary arrangements to go through all the collected remains at another location.

Whether we head back across the desert to meet up with the main convoy or head up into Iraq on the Al Faw where the British are and then cut over to find the 1MEF remains to be seen. The Captain will let us know.

*   *   *

"Shark, what the hell is an *assamitt?*"

"A *what?*" Mark asked Angelo as they sat near their vehicle trying to keep sand out of a morning MRE breakfast somewhere near the Iraq and Kuwait border.

"You know, an *assamitt,*" repeated a frustrated Angelo. "We're driving around and I ask the Captain if we're going to do this or that and he always says 'I don't know, I have to check the *assamitt* on that!'"

"Oh," laughed Mark knowingly, "he's saying azimuth, you dumb ass. You know, like on a compass? It means he has to check with Higher Command to see if that's the direction the operation is going in."

"Oh, you mean that little pointer thing on the compass? Then why doesn't he just say that?"

"He did, in Marine speak."

"What about a... *low density support* set?"

"It means there's a shortage of something."

"Wouldn't it be easier to just say that?"

"Wouldn't it be easier for the enemy to listen in on us if we did?"

"Oh, I see what's going on now."

"Yeah, you see it, but just don't understand it."

* * *

Chef Dante looked up at the knock on his office door just as Dudley stuck his head in.

"Chef?"

"Yes, Dudley..."

"We're kicking ass! Iraqi forces are already in disarray. We're pounding the shit out of them. Shock and awe, baby! Baghdad, Basra, Mosul, Kirkuk, Tikrit, everywhere. The British have already taken the Al Faw peninsula. One of Iraq's Army Divisions surrendered. That's like eight thousand men. Reporters embedded with the fighting units are sending back these incredible pictures of fighting vehicles, tanks, and attack helicopters blowing through southern Iraq. Once we hit Nasiriyah, we're halfway to Baghdad."

"Believe it or not, Dudley, I too have access to all the media. None of this is really news to me. I do keep track of what is going on over there too."

"Then you probably know we lost a helicopter with four Americans and eight Brits, and ten Iraqi missiles landed in Kuwait but we did knock two of them down with Patriot missiles. Anyway, we're on high moral ground, or so claims the President..."

"Very comforting, thanks. Now, back to work."

*　*　*

Emmy was hurrying through the crowded airport terminal with her pilot's case trailing behind her when she heard a newscaster's voice on a nearby bar television and stopped to listen, taking a seat.

"In the Iraq war," reported news commentator Diana Scott in a solemn tone, "the United States today suffered its first major casualties since Operation Iraqi Freedom began. In two separate clashes near the central Iraq city of Nasiriyah, at least twenty American soldiers are believed to be dead and many more wounded or missing in action. In the first incident, an Army maintenance company apparently took a wrong turn in the early morning hours and was ambushed. Eleven soldiers are dead and the rest of the maintenance company is presently unaccounted for. A few miles away ten Marines were killed when their Amphibious Assault Vehicle was hit by a rocket."

"General Pynchon," asked Diana Scott to the retired General, "we initially received reports directly from Central Command in Qatar that Nasiriyah had already been secured. What do you think happened?"

"Well Diana, not knowing all the specifics, one can only assume that capturing this area amounted to an

Economy of Forces Measure which means we initially confront, control, and then bypass any marginal targets in order to focus on the main targets, which of course are the Republican Guard troop concentrations and Saddam Hussein's regime in Baghdad."

"So we didn't get rid of all the bad guys there?"

"That's not something lead forces normally do," explained General Pynchon. "They push on through, and only fire upon those who might try to stop them along the way. No one on the face of the earth has the firepower to stop the United States military, so the only semblance of attack left for the Iraqis is to try and pick off any stray rear elements, or get in a shot as with this Marine disaster. Normally an RPG wouldn't destroy an armored vehicle, as in this instance."

"Is this just a blip on the radar? An unfortunate but expected cost to make rapid gains in this war?"

"Unfortunate? Yes. Expected? No. Iraqi Army elements are already surrendering in huge numbers and liberated Iraqis in the south are welcoming our military with open arms. Bottom line is, Iraqi citizens are glad we are ending tyranny. There will be sacrifices along the way, but in the end we shall prevail."

Worried, Emmy turned away from the broadcast, and phoned her father in a panic.

"Dad, did you hear what happened? There were Marines who died!"

"I know, honey," he said in a father's calming voice. "Don't worry, it wasn't even his division."

"Are you positive?"

"Mark doesn't ride in one of those vehicles."

"Good. What does he ride in?"

"Something with less armor, a Humvee."

"You're kidding, aren't you?"

"I wish I was."

"You mean to tell me he's over there riding around in a Hummer like guys from a radio station do?"

Emmy sobbed, unable to deal with what it was.

"It is what it is, Emmy. Look, you can't be losing it every time you hear a soldier died," he counseled. "You'll just wind up driving yourself crazy."

"I'm already there!" she claimed through her tears. "There are huge weather delays, I'm on my period, I haven't eaten anything, and my brother is in Iraq riding around in a Hummer while a bunch of crazy Iraqis are trying to shoot him. How does our government expect families to cope with all of this?"

"I wish I knew," admitted her father, being just as helpless as she was. "There's not much consolation in knowing thousands of families in America are going through the exact same thing we are, and some of them are going to get horrible news very soon. Call me selfish, but I never want to be part of that community."

"So, you're selfish about wanting your son to stay alive and don't care what anyone thinks about it? Good, count me in too."

"Where exactly are you calling from?"

"Charlotte. I should be home by Friday."

"Good! We can worry together then."

"I'll look forward to it. Thanks for listening, Dad. I do feel a little better now."

"I love you, baby."

"Love you too. I'll call you again tomorrow."

"Call me every day, wherever you are," her father assured her in his ever calming voice. "I love hearing your voice as much as I possibly can."

* * *

North of the Iraqi border, the Marines rejoined the endless convoy and, stuck in another massive traffic jam, took the opportunity to grab a quick bite.

"You know guys, we just came through southern Iraq and all those people seemed real happy to see us," remembered Mark. "That felt really good. They seemed to have enough food, but they went ape-shit when we gave them MREs in that town, what was it called?"

"Safwan, something like that" offered Sykes.

"Safwan, right. But what they really needed was fresh water. Somebody told me Saddam's men came into town and destroyed all the pumps a few days ago. Now why would they do that to their own people?"

"I don't know, man, maybe so that we couldn't get any," offered Valdespino, shaking his head. "There wasn't any electricity either, and it seemed like they got their water, washed their food, and relieved themselves all in the same general area."

"My Dad," related Mark, "thinks this war is completely wrong because it's not being waged for the right reasons. But when I see a place like that little town in the year 2003, and see how they're begging for people like us to come in and help change things, I can see we are here for all the right reasons. Saddam has these big palaces all over this country, and the people out here are living like in medieval times."

"Well spoken, Sebastian. At ease!" said Captain Dylan as he appeared around the AAV where they were sitting. He crouched down with them. "That helicopter accident was rattling for all of us, but when we're attached to Mortuary Affairs that's the way it's going to be. Luckily, my driver got us back to the main convoy."

"Just give me an open road and an *assamitt* and I'll take you home every time!" promised Angelo.

"I have complete confidence in that," smiled the Captain before turning serious. "Now here's what's happening: Some Marines have been killed in Nasiriyah. Mortuary Affairs has been cleared to take the fast lane to reach there by morning. We are heading into an area of very intense resistance. Three battalions of Marines are now fighting in Nasiriyah and we should expect to experience heavy fire. Good to go?"

"GOOD TO GO, CAPTAIN!"

"Head 'em up and move 'em out! Rawhide!"

"You heard the Captain! RAWHIDE!" screamed the First Sergeant, startling everyone into action.

* * *

MARK'S JOURNAL:

The problem with Nasiriyah was in having to pass through it in order for Marines to go up the east side of the Euphrates River to Baghdad and also cross the Tigris at Al Kut so we could secure the western flank. The Third Army bypassed Nasiriyah because they didn't have to cross the river, so it essentially became a Marine operation. At some point, the bad guys decided certain parts of the convoy were susceptible to attack and struck.

We reached the outskirts of Nasiriyah in the early morning hours and there's no way I can accurately describe what happened because there are no words that can ever duplicate the actual experience.

The closer we got to Nasiriyah the more obvious it became that we were definitely entering a hot zone. Artillery and gunfire was constant and the predawn sky was lit up every minute or so with flashes from explosions. Nasiriyah wasn't the front, but it was a flashpoint and the skies were filled with smoke. Since it was near the Euphrates River there were lots of marshes and the roads were pretty bad with muddy choke points where you had to slow way down in order to get through the muck. We'd been warned that if anything moved suspiciously along the way that we should just terminate them, without prejudice.

Attack helicopters were flying above and the road was lined with our tanks and personnel carriers. Closer to the city we could hear incoming small arms and mortar fire and after we crossed one of the bridges the concentration of tanks and Marines increased dramatically. The Captain told us we were now officially in Ambush Alley, a six-mile stretch of hell where the convoy had been taking fire for days.

We had to drive through this area in order to get where MA needed to go and Marines were wall-to-wall, meaning they were flat on the ground with M-16s trained in either direction on the road. Tanks lined the roads and were at every corner. It was tense shit and there was steady incoming fire. There is always a fine point between driving too slow where you're an easy target and moving too fast where you might endanger other Marines, but Angelo got us through it just fine.

The destination ambush point was not a good sight for any of us to see. Directly ahead, a Marine AAV with ten men aboard had been hit by some kind of rocket at the worst possible point in the vehicle's hull. The wreckage was a total burnout and all the Marines aboard probably died instantly where they were sitting, without any warning. I don't know if anyone can take comfort in that. They still died by explosion and fire and the bodies were burned almost beyond recognition.

Over here we all must think about how we'd like to die if we ever have to, and whether or not it's better to have a quick death that burns you up or blows you into a hundred pieces; rather than being a pretty corpse who dies slowly and in a lot of pain. I know it may sound sick to others that we even think about it; but that's the reality of life and death here in Iraq. No one wants to die, but it won't matter to me how or why, whether it's in a firefight or accidentally. Anytime an American serviceman dies it is simply a tragedy.

The bodies were all wrapped neatly in American flags in an area not far from the AAV. The whole area was heavily fortified and we pulled in to form an interior defense so MA could do what they had to. It was really comforting to have a bunch of M1A1 Abrams tanks ringed around us but bullets were still flying everywhere and more RPGs were always a possibility so we were all aware that keeping ourselves protected at all times was a very smart thing to do.

We stayed in Nasiriyah all day and night, which seemed like an eternity, watching firefights flare-up all over the city and always hoping they didn't spread our way. It sure wasn't a night where anyone would get much sleep. Larry, Angelo, and Sykes all wrote letters home when they weren't on watch. Even Captain Dylan was writing when I passed by him on my way back from taking a piss behind a tank near the river.

It wasn't the right environment for writing to Mom and asking her what she did on her first birthday that I've ever missed since being alive. To make matters worse, we found out earlier that thousands of chemical weapon suits and gas masks had been found inside a hospital in Nasiriyah. The Iraqis didn't have these suits because they were afraid we were going to use something against them, so the truth had to be they were getting ready to use some shit against us and hadn't got the chance yet. If they hit us tonight, if this was just a set-up for some massive chemical attack in an area where a large group of our best forces were concentrated, we'd have to be ready for it, but the result probably wouldn't be very nice for anyone involved.

Seven Marine vehicles had been lost in the past few days in and around Nasiriyah, including tanks, armored personnel carriers, and Humvees. A couple were abandoned in the mud and would be retrieved, but the rest had been shot up. One was by friendly fire from one of our A-10 WartHogs. You never like to hear about friendly fire accidents. Never.

Marines and all the other services practice Blur Force Tracking, either through each service branch or Central Command in order to track friendly troop movements so fewer incidents happen. But in a battle zone like we're in, anything can and will happen.

Marines had gone on the offensive and were now moving house to house and building to building throughout Nasiriyah to wipe the enemy out. We'd given Saddam's supporters the opportunity to let us pass through without trying to stop us, and they'd decided to try and sucker-punch us instead. That doesn't work with the Marines, Army, Navy, or Air Force. Oppose us, we will kill you. Hide from us, we will find you. Work with us, we will work with you. In the end, there really are few other options for an enemy.

I thought the last entry would be my last for a while, but First Sergeant Ralston just told us we were to head north, presumably where there are more Marine casualties since that's our support mission. As bad as Nasiriyah is, at least there are a lot of Marines and tanks here. We don't know exactly where we're headed, but I think it is safe to say we are going to get real close to wherever the front is, much quicker than we expected.

We are excited since we are Marines and want to be at the heart of the action; but the closer we get to Baghdad the closer we get to their best fighters and the danger that chemical weapons will be used against us.

*   *   *

From a comfortable recliner, eighty year old ex-Marine Marcus Sebastian frowned at the television program he was watching. Around him in the room were family pictures including wife Emily, sons Ray and Dante, and grandchildren Mark and Emmy; among others. Military photos and awards decorated the walls.

"General Pynchon, we have been receiving very conflicting accounts about what is actually going on in Iraq," began Diana Scott. "Central Command continues to report one thing while reporters embedded with military units are saying something else, and some credible Arab news sources have a completely different spin on the events. Whom do we believe?"

"In a war," explained the General, "things never are completely what they seem to be. We claim to have taken Nasiriyah but we're still engaged in an ongoing firefight there. Several members of an ambushed Army maintenance unit are missing in action. We can expect similar news inconsistencies throughout this war. The Marines are now focused on Nasiriyah and will clear out any resistance. That is a fact, and it is not in doubt."

"It was also reported the British had secured Basra, but there are no British soldiers actually inside the city of Basra, and the fight for control of the Al Faw Peninsula is still being waged a week after it was reported the area was completely secured."

"Look, if the British storm into Basra and just level it a lot of innocent people will die," continued the

General. "Sure, there are some very bad guys in there, as there are anywhere Saddam operates, but we're not going to incur more than acceptable civilian casualties."

"So, control of the area is not in question?"

"Absolutely not. They can't get supplies in, and the bad guys won't get out of there alive."

"Isn't that wishful thinking? We've been led to expect the Iraqi people would rise up against Saddam's regime once we invaded, but it hasn't happened yet."

"These poor people have lived for decades under perhaps the most ruthless dictator in the world," pointed out General Pynchon. "Until they know Saddam and his operatives are dead and there will be no retribution for them to express their views, they're obviously going to be intimidated to take up arms against their oppressors unless they're protected."

"One of your fellow retired military leaders has suggested the Military, the Pentagon, and perhaps even the Secretary of Defense and the President have underestimated the effect of this invasion," she inquired. "We've encountered more resistance than expected, and since we haven't as yet engaged the elite Republican Guard units, this suggests that Saddam's *Fedayeen* paramilitary fighting units are far more deadly than expected. How big of a problem is this?"

"In the whole scope of the conflict, it's merely a temporary annoyance," assured the General. "Saddam's *Fedayeen* are soldiers who are dressing up as civilians in order to blend in with the local populace, often forcing locals to be human shields so they can hit us when we least expect it. They can annoy us, but they have no way of stopping us. We're already less than a hundred miles from Baghdad. There will be casualties along the way. It is the price you pay to wage war. But the enemy facing us cannot possibly win this fight."

Diana paused as news was being relayed to her.

"We're getting reports a Marine support group has suffered casualties somewhere south of Baghdad."

"Not to worry. Keep in mind, Diana, a Marine support group, unlike say an Army support group, is no different than front-line Marines. All Marines are trained as riflemen first, so all Marines or their units can be integrated into any battlefield scenario," explained General Pynchon. "If you compare this to the Army maintenance group like the one ambushed in Nasiriyah a few days ago, the main difference is that Army support groups have some weapons but have had only basic training in how to fight. Marines are extremely well trained, every single one of them all the way down to the cooks and mechanics. If you take them on, there are virtually no weaknesses to exploit."

"Thank you, General. We'll be back soon."

Shaking his head, Marcus changed back to the basketball game just as his favorite nurse Flo walked in with her big blonde beehive hairdo to make his bed. He winked at her as she leaned over to straighten the sheets, checking out her assets in the process with his still keen and ever wandering eyes.

"How are you feeling this morning, Marcus?' Flo asked in a cheerful voice.

"Better, now that you're here to stir me up!"

"Whatever makes you happy," she sighed.

"Exactly what I like to hear!" he smiled.

* * *

MARK'S JOURNAL:

So far, Mortuary Affairs has been keeping us much busier than we have wanted to be. After leaving

Nasiriyah we headed north but heavy fire up ahead slowed us down. Just a couple of days ago a Marine accidentally stepped on an unexploded cluster bomb and lost his life. Then a UH-1 Huey crashed, killing three Marines. The crash scene was not in a secure area so it got more than a little hairy there. We had a lot of air support to keep the Iraqis away so I didn't have to fire my weapon. In fact, I haven't had to fire it at all yet. I don't know whether I should like that or not, but I remain ready just in case, or frosty as they say.

Later that same day two more Marines died and we had to head back toward Nasiriyah to handle it. We were passed by some units heading northeast toward Al Kut and they told us there was another big firefight in Nasiriyah but more units were reaching the area so their company was being sent on ahead. One of the Marines who died got hit by a Humvee while trying to evade Iraqi machine gun fire. The other Marine drowned when his vehicle overturned into a canal.

We keep talking about how it's more than a little unnerving to be going here and there, back and forth, whenever a Marine dies. Someone has to do it, we know that, but we just don't know where we're going most of the time, or what we'll find when we get there. We were positioned south of Diwaniyah and hoping to head for Al Kut where the Republican Guard's Baghdad Division was coming to fight.

But other than at Nasiriyah we haven't seen any evidence that American forces have been losing much equipment or troops. We have seen a lot of dead Iraqi tanks, trucks; and more importantly a lot of dead Iraqi soldiers. There's no word of any chemical weapons being used against us; but as their situation becomes more desperate they might pull out all the stops.

It was a pretty bad scene for us today. An M1A1 Abrams tank drove right into the Euphrates River when a stray bullet killed the driver. None of the other three crew members aboard could get out before it sank upside down and they all drowned. We try not to spend too much time visualizing how families will react when they hear how their loved ones actually died, but you have to wonder what loved ones must think when they get all the details. *What? He got hit by one of our Humvees? His helicopter went down, but not from enemy fire? How could my son have possibly drowned? He was an excellent swimmer!*

Again, anytime anyone dies, tragedy outweighs the details. Sometimes we think about it too much, but it's hard to ignore reality when right in the middle of it.

April 2003

At a camp north of Nasiriya, Valdespino ran up happily with a letter he received.

"Angelo, do you have any cigars left?"

"Not for you, dude."

"Come on, man, I'm a father now!" announced Valdespino. "Look, I got pictures."

Mark and Sykes hurried over to look at the pictures the very proud and grinning father was holding. Angelo reluctantly joined them.

"Congratulations, Larry!"

"I would like to introduce you to Felix Augusto Valdespino, our first American born Cuban, and a future Marine around the year 2022 or so."

"He's as funny looking as you are, Larry!"

"Thanks, he is quite handsome. We named him after his Grandfathers. He was born on March thirteenth. Damn, I wish I could've been there!"

"Is your wife okay?" asked Sykes.

"She's doing great. Here's a picture of her."

"Who are all those people around the bed?"

"Shark, we have a very big family. My wife wrote to say our baby is so beautiful she wants us to, you know, make another one as soon as I get home."

"All right, Larry!" congratulated Sykes.

"What about that cigar, Angelo?"

"Okay, but I'm saving my last one for Baghdad, and from what I'm hearing over the Captain's radio, Marines will be in Baghdad by the end of the week."

"Shock and awesome, baby!" crowed Sykes.

"Meaning, we might just be going home sooner rather than later," predicted Angelo.

The four Marines exchanged high-fives and continued congratulating the new father.

* * *

Chef Dante glanced into the Assistant Executive Chef's office as he passed by, then stopped and went back for another look. Dudley was slumped over his desk, close as he could be to being passed out snoring.

"Dudley…"

"What'd I do?" he wondered, looking guilty.

"Are you all right?"

"I think so. Why?"

"You look like…. Are you hung over?"

"It's not what you think, Chef. I stayed up really late watching the news. Knowing Mark's over there it's becoming more addictive than even some of my past problems. Stuff always keeps happening, and for some reason it seems to be when I'm supposed to be asleep."

"I know what you mean."

"Did you hear about that POW Jessica Lynch? Special Forces busted in, rescuing her. Wasn't it great?"

"I'm happy for her and her family."

"Seals, Rangers, and Marines went in and broke her out, guns blazing."

"You mean you didn't see the video?"

"There was a video?"

"You didn't stay up late enough. Somehow they managed to have a video crew along for the raid."

"No shit?" Dudley was immediately suspicious.

"Well, I don't know if there wasn't any of that," confessed Chef Dante. "They hit the ground running and tracer bullets were firing everywhere. But the funny thing was, no one was shooting back."

"What are you saying?"

"Well, doesn't it seem funny to you when media people are claiming the war isn't going well and we're taking too many casualties, that the Pentagon releases this feel-good story?" suggested Mark's father. "I'm not saying I agree with that assessment of the war's progress since we're less than fifty miles from Baghdad and the Iraqis don't seem to have any way of stopping us, but still, it makes you wonder why they're teasing with promises about having some good news for once."

"My God, you're right!" realized Dudley. "Chef, do you think they're '*Wagging the Dog*' at us?"

"What are they doing to dogs?"

"You know, that movie *Wag the Dog*," Dudley realized. "The premise is that the government hires this famous Hollywood action movie producer to stage a fake war scenario in order to get people's minds off what's really happening there. So, you're saying whoever pulls the strings behind the scenes decided to create a little drama for their own benefit?"

"That is your speculation, not mine."

"Exactly. What I really don't understand about this whole Jessica Lynch thing is they claim she was fighting like a demon before she got wounded and captured, but there don't seem to be any witnesses?"

"Agreed, but any POW who is freed is a hero."

"Chef, if you really do believe in conspiracies, there's a few things I could open your eyes about."

"I would like to open your eyes to the fact we have some quality control problems in our kitchens," pointed out the Executive Chef, getting back to business. "Management does not accept the fact we have little legal control over our union cooks as an excuse for not being able to provide the desired culinary standards to our guests."

"I don't know how to motivate these people."

"Hard to lead those that won't follow orders."

"Do you have any news from Mark?"

"He's not finding many phones where he is."

"Right. Well, I better get back to work."

"Yes, you'd better."

*   *   *

As a dust storm blurred the day outside, Mark sat in his tent writing while fleas crawled over him.

Dear Mom:

I do hope that everything is going well with you. Hopefully I'll be able to call soon. War is war but we're not on the front lines so I guess we're safer than we could be. We usually have enough to eat even though our supply lines are stretched a little thin, especially with what my unit does. Angelo asked me to say hello. As a Marine I think he's about as good as they come.

I haven't killed anyone and from what we hear the war is going pretty well, so I'm sure both of those things will make you feel good. I can't really tell you where we are or what we're doing except we're south of Baghdad and doing our job as best we can.

I told you about my friend Hilario Valdespino from Miami, the guy we call Larry? His wife just had a baby and he mentioned they were trying to find a house. Since you and Herb are in real estate in West Palm Beach, maybe you might come across something in the area that might be in their price range, which probably isn't very much. It's not a problem if you can't help but it's worth a shout out to you anyway.

Sorry I missed your birthday for the first time in my life. Hopefully it won't ever happen again.

Angelo, really surprised me by revealing he's got this young lady back in Chicago named Terri that he wants to settle down with after he gets home. She sounds really great but I'm still trying to figure out what she sees in him. He tells me all these stories about her, even reads me the letters he writes her before he sends them. I do hope I find my own Terri someday.

We're getting ready to pull out so I have to go.

I love you, and hope to talk to you soon.

Mark

* * *

In the expansive living room of their lavish oceanfront home in Miami, Carmen and Herb Fieldstone were having the first of their evening cocktails while watching the news. Newscaster Diana Scott was sitting across from General Pynchon.

"As American military forces push through to Baghdad as an unstoppable force," began Diana Scott, "aren't hasty critics of the American war plan starting to look a bit foolish now?"

"Many of my retired colleagues are eating their words right about now," chuckled General Pynchon a bit smugly. "The war plan has turned out to be brilliant. Let's look at the map here. We've traveled more than three hundred miles through Iraq in a classic multiple pronged attack along the Euphrates River. Marines are now on the eastern and western banks of the Tigris, and the Army and Marines basically own everything in-between. A couple of days ago Marines virtually destroyed the entire Baghdad and Medina divisions of the Republican Guards at Al Kut, captured thousands of prisoners, and right now there are so many Marines on the outskirts of Baghdad it must really be terrifying for what's left of Saddam's regime."

"We have reports of many thousands of Iraqi civilians fleeing the capital and actual video of Saddam International Airport being seized by American forces," added Diana Scott. "Over four hundred Iraqi soldiers were killed when American forces captured the airport, apparently without a single American casualty. Can those numbers possibly be accurate?"

"Absolutely! War is a chess match and once you learn the enemy's strategy, checkmate is just a matter of time. You don't lose many pieces in the process."

Diana Scott paused as more news came in.

"We are just now getting reports from embedded reporters that lead elements of the First Marine Expeditionary Force have entered Baghdad from the Southeast and are engaged in heavy fighting. What is your assessment of this, General?"

"My assessment is that the Iraqis are in a world of hurt because there are no armed forces on the face of this earth that would fare very well in combat with United States Armed Forces."

* * *

MARK'S JOURNAL:

We are near Diwaniyah and are getting ready to move out. The last few days have been like many of those before them. Marines die and we go there to help make sure their remains are preserved. Would we rather be up past Al Kut and heading for Baghdad? No doubt.

Sometimes it's hard to keep focus on the latest Marine who has died. Like the one yesterday who fell when a mortar round hit his AAV. He was in so many pieces that the MA guys had to go around with those little red flags and mark the spots where parts of his body were before collecting them all. Of course we care but as hard as it is to admit, we're all starting to get used to people dying. Does it make me a better Marine? Am I getting stronger, more hardened, or have I seen enough death where I'm beginning to take it in stride?

We hear the war might be starting to wind down. If that happens Marines will probably be the first to be sent home since we're not trained to be peacekeepers. Nothing could make me happier.

*　　*　　*

On the road between Diwaniyah and Al Kut the convoy passed through a small town not even on the map. Like most of Iraq they'd seen there was no running water or electricity and the buildings looked as if they were ready to crumble from the vibration of the trucks and vehicles passing through on the narrow road.

It was very early in the morning and only a few citizens cautiously poked their heads out to see who was making all the noise. A few smiled and waved but Mark didn't wave back. Something was in the air today. He could sense it, feel it, and almost smell it.

The convoy had just cleared the main area of town when bullets began flying. An RPG flew over the top of the Humvee's hood, missing by a few feet before exploding into a building on the other side of the road. Angelo gunned the Humvee and Mark started firing.

"Three o'clock!" yelled the Captain, and Mark started firing the machine gun while the words were still hanging in the air. Mark could see where the fire was coming from and tore up a building about a hundred and fifty yards away where the Iraqis were shooting from. The rest of the convoy also opened up as bullets began hitting vehicles from all directions. Mark kept firing on anything that moved. The Captain called for air support, and in minutes the convoy cleared the town and the firefight began to wind down from the Marines withering arsenal.

"Cease fire!" shouted the Captain loudly and Mark immediately stopped firing. His breath was rapid, his hands were shaking, and his eyes did not trust their surroundings. Angelo slowed the Humvee to a halt and the Captain was calling down the line to assess the situation. No one was moving in the building Mark had fired on. He searched the farmland around where they were now but couldn't find anyone moving anywhere.

All the way down the convoy Marines were in defensive positions while others were in the process of performing damage assessments. A medic was up on First Sergeant Ralston's Humvee already tending to Sykes, who had been wounded in the upper arm. An RPG had hit the back of a supply truck but no medics were there so it didn't appear there were injuries.

Within a few minutes, attack helicopters were swooping overhead strafing the town, and an A-10 Warthog flew slowly over the scene to pick off the last remnants of resistance, if there were still any.

The Captain sent out teams to find out if who had been shooting at them were eliminated. Mark and the other gunners were to provide cover fire.

First Sergeant Ralston took four Marines with him to inspect the area Mark had targeted. They moved in cautiously, but whoever had been in the area was either dead or gone now. They entered the building and emerged minutes later carrying weapons retrieved.

The First Sergeant was talking to Captain Dylan on the radio as they started back toward the convoy.

They dropped AK-47s and an RPG launcher on the ground in a pile and soon other Marines were bringing up other weapons they'd found in their searches.

Angelo walked back to check on Sykes, had a word with First Sergeant Ralston, then came back nodding up to Mark as if very impressed.

"You killed the shit out of them, Shark!"

"Everyone's dead in there?"

"Thirteen of the bastards, like a whole baker's dozen. Not one was even left wounded."

"You're kidding me, right?"

"Nice work," complimented the Captain, who'd maintained his usual cool throughout the firefight.

"So where are all the rest of their weapons?"

"That's all they found," said Angelo, looking over to the Captain for support.

"Sebastian, apparently we found there may have been a few non -combatants in there."

"You mean like women and children?"

"There was simply nothing else we could do," the Captain reminded him. "They're using the locals as human shields, thinking we won't fire back. Obviously, that's not going to happen."

"But Captain, I…"

"You did the right thing. We took fire from the enemy and you fired back until the enemy stopped shooting. That RPG only missed by a few feet. If you didn't react quickly and they fired another one, maybe none of us are still alive to be discussing."

"That's right!" seconded Angelo happily. "You might have just saved my life. I owe you one, bro!"

Mark was totally stunned by what had happened and didn't know what to say or think.

*   *   *

"Dad, it's me!" called out Emmy as she walked in the front door of her father's house.

"We're back here in the den!" he called out to her. "Welcome home!"

She rolled her pilot's case off to the side, hung her coat in the hall closet, and headed into the family room. Stephanie and her father were next to each other on the couch watching television.

"Hi Dad, hi Stephanie."

"Hey girl! Good trip?" asked Stephanie.

Emmy gave her father a quick kiss and a hug before collapsing in a chair.

"They're always good when they're finally over." Emmy stared at the screen, trying to figure out what she was seeing there. "What's going on?"

"Marines are in Firdos Square in downtown Baghdad," explained her father. "They just pulled down a big statue of Saddam and now the Iraqi people are celebrating and stomping all over it."

"Does this mean the war is over?"

"Not necessarily. Apparently there's still a lot of fighting going on. Our Army is fighting their Army near the airport and Marines are battling small pockets of resistance in the southeast part of the city."

"Most analysts are saying there's no organized resistance left," mentioned Stephanie.

"Right," agreed Dante. "There's some looting in Baghdad and a lot of bad guys are still there, but if there's anything left of the Republican Guard, they're keeping a pretty low profile."

"Any word on Saddam?" asked Emmy.

"Nope. Might've headed up north to hide."

"I just hope it's over soon," said Emmy, shaking her head. "I wonder how Mark is?"

"Safe and sound is all we hope for. Hungry?"

"Starving! What will you cook for me?"

"Nothing!" said her father. "I've been cooking all day, and I'm tired now. We'll go out for dinner."

"Sounds like a good plan to me."

*   *   *

Captain Dylan's company pulled off to the side of the road just north of Al Kut for a midday break. The traffic on the highway was moving forward very slowly as it was jammed with Marine tanks and vehicles. The landscape all around them was littered with the burned out remains of Republican Guard tanks and vehicles.

"We're less than forty miles south of Baghdad," advised Angelo. "Wish we'd been here a few days ago to kick some Republican Guard ass, but from the look of things our fellow Marines didn't need our help."

"The First Sergeant heard we killed more than a thousand of them here and another twenty five hundred surrendered," related Sykes with a smile. "Plus, there wasn't a single Marine casualty."

"Outstanding! Are you doing okay, Sykes?"

"Just a scratch. I'm luckier than I thought."

"Those *mudderfuggers* ambushed us and got what was coming to them," said Valdespino. "I saw this one guy running from one building to another. He had a gun so I fired. The first shot missed, but the second one got him in the temple. I checked that shit out myself."

"Why couldn't I have lost my cherry back there too?" complained Angelo. "Larry got one, Wichita got at least two, and Shark wasted the whole rest of them. I want to trade off with you and work the big gun for a while. I gotta turn my freaking numbers around fast!"

"Fine with me," replied Mark quietly.

"What exactly is your problem, Shark?"

"I said fine, Angelo."

"Yeah, in your best sad ass pitiful little voice," mocked Angelo. "You've been moping around for the past two days hardly even saying a word to anyone. Do you want us to feel sorry because you killed some innocent civilians too? Don't hold your breath. Would you feel better if one of us got killed back there? Would that make it better for you to swallow?"

"Eat shit, Angelo!"

"Good, that's more like my old school Shark now! You know what else? I don't care how many of these bastards die or who the hell they are! If they're trying to kill us then I hope they all burn! If it was me who killed them instead of you, I'd want the whole freaking world to know about it so that when I got back home all the little children would be telling stories and singing songs about me in the mean streets of Chicago."

"Well, that's the difference between us, isn't it?"

"Angelo, when we get to Baghdad, please find a place to take a bath," suggested Valdespino, changing the subject. "You're getting a little too ripe."

"Am I, Larry? Then maybe you should spend a little less time trying to smell my extremities?"

"You should have taken a bath with us when we were back on the Euphrates," agreed Sykes. "Man, did that ever feel good!"

"Well, if I had done that, then who would've guarded your ugly pale butts while you were out frolicking in the river like some freaking mermen?"

"It was totally safe out there."

"Listen, there's nowhere in Iraq that is totally safe," Angelo corrected Sykes. "Besides, I heard a few guys drowned in that river a few days before. While I'm good at a whole hell of a lot of things, swimming in a bunch of decomposed shit isn't one I want to do."

"Don't you worry Angelo," promised Mark as he stood up to return to their vehicle, "the first chance I get when we get to Baghdad, Uncle Mark is going to take you out shopping and buy you some of those water wings so you can start swimming with the big boys."

"*Really?*" Angelo smiled back childishly. "Well screw you very much, Uncle Shark!"

* * *

An Iraqi bellman pointed out the phone in the hotel lobby to Mark. He hurried over to make his call.

"Hello…"

"Dad!"

"Mark! Where are you?"

"Baghdad. Found a phone that actually works."

"Great! So good to hear your voice! We've been going nuts here not hearing from you for weeks."

"It was a long drive. We got here last night."

"How are you doing?"

"I'm okay I guess…"

"What's wrong?"

"Just the usual war stuff. I'll tell you about it when I get home."

"Looking forward to it, hopefully soon."

"Have the Iraqis officially surrendered?"

"We haven't heard anything, but commentators are saying it's almost over. No one really knows where Saddam is, probably in hiding. What's Baghdad like?"

"It's kind of crazy here, and a whole lot bigger than I thought it was. We camped out at the university. and it's actually pretty quiet around there now, which is nice. Having a lot of Marines around tends to keep the bad guys away. This morning we got a better look around Baghdad and saw how heavily we've bombed them. Not really in any residential areas, mostly just infrastructure and government buildings."

"Right, so what will Marines do in Baghdad when they're finished fighting?"

"We don't know for sure if that's all over yet. A lot of the people here seem to be really glad to see us, but we still see two or three guys at a time walking around glaring at us. We figure they're probably soldiers who ditched their uniforms to stay alive but for now we're just letting them keep walking. There's still some shooting at our forces and a lot of rioting and looting going on. The unit we've been humping for might not have much to do here, at least we hope not, so we might be reassigned to do military policing."

"Just be careful out there…"

"I do it all the time. Listen, we have to get back to our unit or the Captain will start worrying. I'll call again soon as I can. Give my love to everyone."

"I'm happy you called, Mark. You know how very proud of you I am."

"Thanks. Bye Dad, I love you."

*   *   *

Stepping out from the shower and drying off, Emmy walked back into her hotel room as she heard the news reporter's voice on the television.

"At least one Marine is dead and approximately twenty two were wounded," reported the male television commentator, "during a heavy firefight yesterday at the Imam Mosque in downtown Baghdad. Marines were sent to investigate reports that some Iraqi military leaders were suspected to be having a meeting there. When the Marines advanced on the mosque they came under heavy machine gun fire from paramilitary forces. After a nearly hour-long firefight, Marines took control of the mosque and took several fighters into custody along with a weapons cache and explosives. If there were any Iraqi leaders they apparently fled into the surrounding neighborhood during the firefight, prompting more Marine units to go searching house-to-house. There is no word on the number of Iraqi casualties at the mosque."

"Elsewhere in Baghdad, Marines have started to take firm measures to stop the rampant looting in the city which followed the collapse of the Baath Party regime. This widespread plundering included many of Baghdad's national museums containing some of the most prized ancient artifacts in the world. The Marines are also trying hard to persuade Baghdad's police and firefighters to return to their posts, but so far they have refused. We'll be back with more news soon..."

Emmy looked at the phone and thought about calling her Dad, then reconsidered and grabbed a small wine bottle from the mini-bar, drinking straight from it.

*　　*　　*

"All right Devil Dogs," began Captain Dylan as he addressed his company of men in a looted university classroom, "I know you men are anxious for news about what we'll be doing here. The 1MEF is pulling out this morning and heading up the highway to Tikrit, which just happens to be Saddam Hussein's hometown. With Mosul and Kirkuk having fallen, Tikrit is probably the last stand for the Iraqi Army and Saddam's loyalists, and Marines will make their fall complete. Unfortunately, we will not be accompanying them."

Groans reverberated throughout the room.

"I know, but we still have Mortuary Affairs back and we are not going up to Tikrit unless needed. Don't worry, we'll be keeping pretty busy right here in Baghdad. The scene at the mosque the other day was heavy duty and those Marines who died on the bridge only serve to remind us that this is still a very dangerous place. Four Marines were also injured at a checkpoint northeast of here, one of them seriously, when a suicide bomber walked up to them and blew himself up. Saddam's loyalists are still taking potshots at us, but be very careful about returning fire in densely populated civilian areas. I don't like it any better than any of you do. If someone shoots at me I damn well want to shoot back. All I'm asking is to continue exercising good trigger discipline."

"Our engineers are working hard to get water and power back up throughout the city, but what is really needed right now in Baghdad is real law and order," emphasized Captain Dylan. "We are going to stop the looters even if we have to shoot them. We are going to disarm whoever has a weapon, and we will also target any activity promoting terrorism of any kind. As an example, a Marine unit just yesterday raided a building where the Iraqis were packing explosives into children's dolls and also turning motorcycle jackets into suicide bomb carriers. Marines stopped a suspicious man at a checkpoint yesterday and when they searched his briefcase, they found a bomb inside. There are literally tons of weapons in this city. AK-47s, RPGs, mortars, explosives, and more ammunition than the Iraqis could ever possibly need or use. We have to get it out of their hands before they use it against us."

"So until Higher orders us to do differently, we will be going out in teams for the next few days to search areas of Baghdad that our intelligence people are interested in. Everyone will carry an M-16 and wear a helmet and flak jacket, but you can leave your chemical gear in your vehicle. Since they haven't used any on us all the way up here from Kuwait, there's reason to believe they probably won't use chemicals or gas in a densely populated area such as Baghdad. I said probably. There's really no telling what a bunch of crazy, desperate people might do. Good to go?"

* * *

Dudley was slumped in a chair in his living room dressed in underwear and holding a can of beer while watching TV in the wee hours of the morning.

"The tyrant of the world is finished!" announced the Shiite Muslim leader to the cheering crowd outside the mosque. "Thanks to the coalition and thank Allah for Iraq being victorious. God is great. Thanks to Allah for those who have helped end this tyranny!"

"Scenes like this are being repeated all over Iraq," reported a news commentator on the screen, "as organized resistance against Operation Iraqi Freedom ended with the majority of Saddam Hussein's forces giving up the fight after Marines swept through upwards of twenty five hundred Iraqi soldiers in fighting yesterday during the fall of Tikrit."

Dropping his beer, Dudley began snoring away.

* * *

With M-16s in hand, the Marines parked their vehicles at a corner and fanned out through an affluent Baghdad neighborhood in the early morning. Captain Dylan stayed near the vehicles with a few men while four teams headed up four different streets.

Angelo walked up one side of the street, followed by Mark; while Valdespino led the way up the other side of the tree-lined avenue with Sykes close behind. First Sergeant Ralston followed down the middle of the street with a half dozen other Marines.

The First Sergeant motioned to the men when he wanted them to search a particular property. They were to go in and radio back if they found anything suspicious. Mark and Angelo were dispatched down the driveway of an older mansion that appeared to be deserted. They looked inside the windows but could not see anyone or notice anything out of the ordinary.

They moved on to the garage and Angelo jimmied open a door to have a look inside. There was a Mercedes and a BMW; but not any weapons.

"I guess not everyone here is so poor after all."

Angelo kept looking around in the garage while Mark ventured back outside and was surprised to find someone looking directly at him.

A little Iraqi girl, maybe four years old and wearing a blue dress, was watching him from the grass ten feet away. He could tell she was a bit afraid but also a little curious too. She was clutching a doll to her chest with one hand and Mark immediately thought of the Captain's warning about explosives in dolls.

Mark turned the barrel of his gun away and kneeled down to her height. He smiled and she smiled back. She held out a closed fist to give him something.

Angelo emerged from the garage, startling the little girl as much as he startled himself. She was ready to run away but then stopped, smiled at Mark and held her hand out to him again.

"Shark, what the hell are you doing?" asked Angelo with great trepidation. "She has a doll!"

"She wants to give me something," said Mark, not taking his eyes off her.

"Are you crazy? It might be C4!"

"She's just a little girl, Angelo," Mark laughed.

"Whose side is she on? Don't let her get close!"

"Angelo, go wait by the tree if you'll feel safer."

"Don't worry, I will!"

Angelo hurried quickly over to a tree near the back of the property and lit up a smoke.

Mark beckoned to the little girl again and she slowly started to walk closer with a shy little smile on her pretty face. When she got within a few feet she reached out her arm as far as she could and Mark reached out to take what was in her hand. Angelo covered his eyes in anticipation.

"What the hell is taking you clowns so long?" demanded First Sergeant Ralston loudly over the radio, frightening the little girl. She opened her hand, dropped something on the ground, then turned and ran across the yard as fast as she could. She looked back at Mark then disappeared through a hole in the fence to the next yard.

"These are some big estates," Mark radioed back. "We should be through soon."

"Make damn sure of that!"

Mark smiled, reached down to pick up what the little girl dropped, then rose to his feet and headed over to where Angelo was.

"What was it?"

Mark revealed a tiny yellow flower.

"She was just trying to give me a flower."

"I'd still be careful, it could be poisonous."

"I'll take my chances." Mark put the flower in a front pocket. He looked back up and spied something out of the ordinary. "Hey, look back over there!"

Angelo looked where Mark was pointing. At the far end of the estate property stood a tall stone wall with a heavy gate surrounded a small cottage.

"Maybe it's where they keep a crazy Uncle?"

"I don't think so. Let's go take a look."

The closer they got to the old cottage the more their interest was piqued. The gate was butted up almost flush against the walls of the cottage. It took a few minutes for Angelo to pry the gate open, then a minute more to pry the front door which finally creaked open. Musky stale air greeted them as they quickly entered the cottage with rifles pointed. The electricity didn't work and the place didn't look like it had been lived in for a long time. Mark started to check out the rooms.

"Angelo, come over here."

In a small empty bedroom they found a stack of small aluminum boxes.

"What do you think it is?" asked Angelo, ready to fire on anything that moved.

"Don't know, explosives or ammunition?"

"I don't think so," observed Angelo. "They look like metal file boxes. I'll check it out."

"This place is giving me the creeps."

'That little girl was the real creepy one!" replied Angelo with all due seriousness. "Where did she just appear from and where were her parents while she was playing flower girl to a couple of stone cold killers?"

Angelo lifted one of the boxes up, checked the weight and tried to shake the contents.

"Sounds like paper."

Angelo set his rifle down and produced a wire to use on the box lock on the box. He got it open and was speechless as he looked inside the box.

"What is it?"

"The root of all evil!" Angelo exclaimed in joy.

Angelo handed the box over to Mark and quickly started picking the lock on another.

"It's money, American currency!"

Angelo found the same contents in another box.

"Shark, there has to be a hundred thousand dollars in each box. There are, let's see, like twenty-two boxes here. That's over two million dollars!"

Angelo picked up a ten thousand dollar bundle.

"What are you doing?"

"Finders keepers, losers weepers! Quick, take some of it now until I figure out a way to come back for the rest later. Come on, hurry up!"

"No! We couldn't possibly keep this a secret."

"We can get ten grand in our underwear!"

"The only thing we can both do is wind up getting court-martialed for stupidity."

Mark switched on his radio as Angelo looked up to the heavens with closed eyes, unable to believe what his friend and fellow Marine was about to do.

"First Sergeant, you need to get some people down to the cottage at the rear of this property right away! You are not going to believe what we found."

"On our way!" promised Ralston.

"Shark, you will probably never know just how extremely disappointed I am in you right now," vowed Angelo sadly as he very reluctantly returned the money to the box after Mark turned his radio off.

"I had some high hopes for you, but you've chosen to make the ultimate mistake of being an honest man. This is absolutely incredible! I won't even be able to tell anyone the story. It's just too mortifying!"

* * *

MARK'S JOURNAL:

I was actually slightly tempted to take some of the loot but just like Angelo I claimed otherwise when Captain Dylan asked us the question later. He said it was human nature to be tempted by the cash, but better judgment prevailed so he was proud of us. Angelo claimed it never even crossed his mind to take the money, but confided he was a little worried about what I might do. I hope the Captain knows us both better than that. The Captain told us later a lot of well-off Iraqis hoarded U.S. currency in case they ever had to flee the country. It's unclear who owned the property but we also found a weapons cache in the same neighborhood so it turned out to be a very productive search mission for our company.

The next day we got word the Fourth Army was coming into Baghdad next week and all Marines would be leaving. We don't know where we're going yet, but leaving Baghdad is cool with us. If the fighting is over then our job here is over too. The Army is better equipped mentally for police work, although we have heard a citizen's group called the Free Iraqi Forces are also supposed to help start patrolling in Baghdad soon.

We haven't had much to do Mortuary Affairs, which is very good news from an operational standpoint. There was an incident the other day though that I still just don't understand. A Marine was shot and killed by his own unit because he was mistaken for an Iraqi. How could it possibly happen? Someone is going to have a much worse guilt trip than I do. If I shot one of my own guys I couldn't think of living any more.

Some Marines who went up to Tikrit told us the 1MEF pulled up about two hundred and fifty vehicles, which is a pretty formidable fighting force of maybe fifty tanks, plus Cobras and F/A-18 Hornets. Supposedly, about twenty five hundred Iraqis were guarding the city but they didn't want to fight and ran away, abandoning their vehicles and stripping off their uniforms when the going got tough. A Marine would never ever do that, regardless of the odds he faced. We know there are a lot of Iraqi soldiers everywhere who have retired into their civilian clothes for safety. They're still somewhat of a threat if they reorganize, but interrogating every Iraqi and searching their homes can't be done, at least not by us.

I called Emmy and my Mom and Uncle Ray. Emmy was hyperventilating; she was so surprised to get a call from me. We had a good cry together, which is all right because she's the only person I'll ever let myself cry around. Mom was a total trip. She was having a party and just started shrieking when she heard it was me. Mom is very dramatic, which is why I'm glad I'm more like my Dad, who's definitely not. Uncle Ray was of course, way over the top as usual. He told me how this victory ranked up there with the greatest military campaigns in history, and how I could always be proud of that; as opposed to his experience in Vietnam where the brass tied their hands and didn't let them win the war. I've heard that same story about fifty times now.

* * *

Dante stared at the tv, dressed for work but not ready to leave until he finished his morning coffee.

"General, what about these so-called Weapons of Mass Destruction?" asked Diana Scott. "Why haven't we found any trace of them yet?"

"It's just a matter of time, Diana, and time is all about having patience. This is a big country and there are a lot of isolated areas where this stuff might be. I don't think it's a question of *if* we find anything; it's simply a matter of *when*. We know they were continuing to manufacture banned substances and were obviously hiding something from the U.N. Weapons Inspectors or they would've complied with the terms set forth. We've found chemical suits in many places. Iraqis know we don't use chemical weapons, so it's obvious they were planning to use them against us."

"Then there is the real question that begs to be asked," replied Diana Scott. "Why, if they had chemical weapons and were planning to use them, didn't they in fact use them against coalition troops?"

"I can only assume," proposed the General, "our advance through the country was so swift it left the Iraqis disorganized and unable to communicate orders down through their chain of command."

"General, what if we never find evidence of any Weapons of Mass Destruction, would that somehow invalidate the necessity for going to war in Iraq?"

"Not in my view. We've seen and heard from the Iraqi people themselves how badly they were oppressed by this tyrant. They've welcomed American liberators with open arms. With good intelligence tying Saddam Hussein's regime to funding terrorist groups like Al Qaeda, the reasons for the war are above questioning, and far beyond any reproach."

"Thank you, General."

Shaking his head, Dante headed off to work.

* * *

Dante answered the phone in his office.

"This is Chef Sebastian. Can I help you?"

"Yes, get me out of here!" shouted Mark.

"Mark! I was wondering when you were going to get around to calling me again. You seem to have called everyone else you know!"

"I just wanted to let you know we're leaving Baghdad. Well, actually in about a minute or two."

"What's up?"

"The Fourth Army is coming to relieve us. We're not really peacekeepers like they are."

"Does it mean you might be coming home?"

"Sounds good to me but they haven't told us anything yet. I don't know what other use they'd have to keep all us Marines here."

"Where are they sending you?"

"Looks like we'll be going down to Al Kut for a while. It's about forty miles southeast of Baghdad. The Marines are taking over a former Republican Guard Army garrison. Supposed to have phone and Internet service so you'll probably hear from me more often."

"I can live with that."

"I thought so. I'll call once we get settled."

"Great. I love you, Mark."

"Right back at you, Dad. Bye…"

*   *   *

MARK'S JOURNAL:

Our new home in Al Kut really isn't all that bad. It is cramped and primitive and definitely nowhere near up to par with American military bases, but it is nice to have a roof over your head and a cot to sleep in for a change. Higher command brought in a mess kitchen so we won't have to eat any more MREs for a while.

Everyone's been mellowing out for a few days and catching up on their sleep, but the Captain always comes up with something to keep us alert or busy. We're kind of retrofitting the base to fit our needs, so it's a welcome change of pace from what we've been doing. Mortuary Affairs is here too and I think they also like having something else to do than their normal job.

Then just when we thought nothing bad was going to happen again, it did. There's a firing range not far from here where some Marines were practicing with a rocket propelled grenade launcher. Something went wrong, we don't know exactly what it was yet, but the grenade exploded in the tube. There were more little flags on the ground than I would ever like to remember. Three Marines died and seven were wounded pretty badly. These guys thought they'd made it through the war and were on their way home. Their families were probably figuring the same thing. Then something like this happens and it freaks you out to know that as long as you're over here, anything can happen at any time.

May 2003

A group of nearly a hundred Marines were gathered around a tv monitor at the Al Kut military base. On the screen was the picture of an aircraft carrier and a Navy plane was landing on it. The plane rolled to a halt and two pilots emerged from the cockpit.

The camera revealed the co-pilot was none other than President Bush. A cheer went up from the Marines as his identity was revealed. Wearing a flight jacket, the Commander-in-Chief walked up to a podium full of microphones as the servicemen on deck cheered. Behind was a banner reading Mission Accomplished.

"Major combat operations in Iraq have ended," announced the President to prolonged cheers from the carrier crew and the Marines at Al Kut. "In the battle of Iraq the United States and our allies have prevailed and now our coalition is engaged in securing that country. In this battle we have fought for the cause of liberty and for the peace of the world."

"Our nation and our coalition are proud of this accomplishment, yet it is the members of the United States military who achieved it," said the President. "Your courage, your willingness to face danger for your country and for each other made this day possible. Because of you the tyrant has fallen, and Iraq is free."

More cheers and high-fives were exchanged.

"Operation Iraqi Freedom was carried out with a combination of precision and speed and boldness the enemy did not expect, and the world had not seen before," continued the President. "Marines and soldiers charged into Baghdad across three hundred fifty miles of hostile ground in one of the swiftest advances of heavy arms in history. You have shown the world the skill and might of the American armed forces. No device of man can remove tragedy from war, yet it is a great advance when the guilty have far more to fear from the war than the innocent. The battle of Iraq is one victory in a war on terror that began on September 11, 2001 and still goes on. Thank you for serving our country and our cause."

The cheering Marines continued to holler as Angelo stepped up to address the President's image.

"You're welcome, Mr. President! Now when do we get to go home?"

Angelo succeeded in getting louder cheers from the Marines than the President did.

*   *   *

Wearing a halter top and shorts, Emmy was stretched out on a sofa in her hotel room enjoying a glass of wine as the television focused on Diana Scott.

"Gentlemen, along with all our viewers we have just experienced a war full of surprising developments which has come to an unexpectedly quick end on a very positive note for the United States military. General, where do we both go from here?"

"Iraq is going to move from a brutal dictatorship into a democracy of free elections, law and order for its people, and the opportunity to modernize their entire infrastructure," predicted the General on a very positive note. "There will of course be some isolated pockets of resistance along the way and some transitional systems may still need to be refined, but there's no doubt in my mind the future of Iraq is far brighter today than it ever was. And that is all due to the brave men and women of our Armed Forces and the Bush Administration."

"Diana, if I may?"

"Yes, Congressman Ballantree."

"I've known Fitz Pynchon a long time and he's one of the few retired Generals who didn't second guess the war planning or our ability to actually get the job done," began the Congressman. "So we have to give him credit for at least that. But the General misses the point of where these two disparate countries are actually going. The Iraqi people need to know the United States is a liberator and not an occupying force. We must give the Iraqi people the necessary tools to build a democracy of their own choosing and not ours. If we don't succeed in doing this, Saddam Hussein might be the least of our worries in Iraq."

"Mr. Al Khayyam, you seem amused by this?"

"It is easier to laugh than to cry, Miss Scott. First, let me say that as an Arab I am pleased to see Saddam Hussein removed from power. Despots are never good for the people under their thumb. I also agree with what the General has said, except for this inherent validation that the United States somehow has the moral right to make these determinations for Iraq. I also agree with what Congressman Ballantree has said, except for the assumption Iraqi people are already not seeing the United States as an occupying force. Who but the United States believes the Iraqi people actually want their help to form a new government?"

"Unfortunately," summarized General Pynchon, "Mr. Khayyam's always narrow viewpoint underlies the perpetual distrust in the Arab world for anything that a western democracy does. Also a prime reason why their countries stay in the dark, surrounded by turmoil."

"Come on, Fitz," countered Ballantree, "if we are ever going to effectively operate in the Arab world we have to better understand their cultures, accept why they have reason to distrust us, and stop committing judgment errors with our policies so these countries can choose their own self-determination."

"Congressman, thank you.," applauded Mr. Al Khayyam. "The American government is actually the entity which has the narrow viewpoint of the rest of the world because they only see things in the way it supports their agenda. America invaded Iraq for no good reason and won the war quickly. I don't think anyone would have bet against this outcome, even Saddam Hussein. But in Arab eyes the fact remains the United States ignored all the united governing bodies of the world with a pre-emptive strike before a supposed enemy had the means and opportunity to attack them. Very effective strategy. I believe the last time this tactic was employed was on September 11, 2001 in America."

"That was an abominable act of terror, not some pre-emptive strike!" roared the General. "I have never heard of a bigger, smellier pile of crap before in my entire life! How dare you make that comparison?"

"So what it is you're saying, Mr. Al Khayyam," pressed on Diana Scott, "is Al Qaeda knew that with hard-line conservative Republicans taking over the White House, they felt the United States was going to come after them no matter what, so they struck first?"

"Like it or not, this is exactly how much of the Arab world sees it," confirmed Al Kyahham.

"Good Gawd!" roared a visibly angry General Pynchon, unable to control his emotions. "Do all of you people perpetually have your heads up your rear ends?"

The three men began arguing vehemently. The show's host was at a loss to control them.

"Three Voices will continue shortly...hopefully."

* * *

Mark and Angelo were sitting outside on lounge chairs, bare-chested in the hot sun, wearing sunglasses and sipping bottled water as they enjoyed an easy day at their new home in Al Kut while flies buzzed around.

"Some people would rather be sitting by a pool in Las Vegas today," reflected Angelo, "but not me. I'm very happy to be right here."

"I completely agree," nodded Mark. "We've got the beach all around us but we don't have to deal with lots of cool water and all the tanned skin and teeny bikinis, plus all those cold beers and cocktails we'd be forced to drink. Yes sir, this really is the life…"

"Mail call! Cicci! Sebastian!"

"Thank you, Santa!" said Angelo gratefully as he was inundated with letters and packages. Mark was given his own fair share, although it was less than a third of what Angelo received.

"A letter from my Mama, another letter from my Mama," began Angelo, "one from my Nonna, a letter from one of my brothers, and oh yeah, a letter from sweet Terri! Looks like I'll be up late tonight…"

"Even for a Marine, you're a real pig," observed Mark. "Four letters from my Dad, which is amazing in that he could find the time to write this much. Twelve, no fourteen letters from my Mom, which is a little on the light side for her. Four from my sister, one from my Aunt and Uncle, one that looks like it's from Grandpa, and one from an old girlfriend who cheated on me. Like I really care if she's sorry about it now…"

"My brother says my nephew Rocco is tearing it up in little league," reported Angelo. "He's going to be a major leaguer someday. I know talent almost better than anyone and this kid is the real deal. Two letters total from Poppa, both on official funeral home stationary I might add. Even a letter from my priest."

"You go to church?" Mark seemed astonished by the very thought of it. "A heathen like you?"

"I'm Catholic, so it's not like I have a choice."

"What's this?" wondered Mark opening a large envelope. "From St. Helena, California. Angelo, I have just received an invitation to join the CIA."

Angelo's eyes flashed open wide.

"No freaking way! If they're going to make a spook out of anyone here, then it should be me."

"Relax, it's from the Culinary Institute of America where you learn to become a Chef."

"Did your Dad send you that?"

"I doubt it. My Dad's not pushy like that. This was probably Dudley's idea. He's an alumnus."

"So while you're learning how to make a primo marinara sauce, which my mother could teach you for a hell of a lot cheaper than those people could," said Angelo, "I'm working on some big plans of my own. When I get home I'm going to use my Veterans loan to buy a house somewhere cheap, sell it fast and then travel around and see how many times I can get laid."

"I thought you were going to marry Terri?"

"That's later…"

"What about our night club gig in Las Vegas?"

"That's later too," intimated Angelo. "It's going to take me a few months of intense sexual indiscretion to remove each month of abstinence I've suffered over here while heroically defending my country. Let my example lead you, young Shark."

"I'll pass. My future when I get home is to be a big fat cat laying around just eating and sleeping."

"Look at all these magazines. Time, Newsweek, US News & World Report, even People. We're over here fighting this war and they know more about what's going down than we do. So that's how we did it so quickly? Now I see."

"What do you mean?"

"A bunch of reporters were embedded with the forward units to show the war up close and personal," continued Angelo. "They were sending pictures back home live from the battlefield using these videophones and shit. Why didn't they assign one of those dudes to follow us around?"

"Central Command really wouldn't want any reporters following units like Mortuary Affairs around," commented Mark, pointing out the obvious. "Dead American servicemen in many pieces are not the ideal war coverage most people want to see back home."

"Roger on that, Shark."

*   *   *

Captain Dylan was just finishing a presentation to the Marines in the base mess hall when Angelo raised his hand from the audience.

"Captain, can I have permission to speak?"

"What is it, Private First Class Cicci?"

"Well, The men and I are wondering if you've heard anything about us going home."

The Captain paused, looked down momentarily, then nodded his head. "Yes, I have."

A loud cheer went up throughout the mess hall.

"As you all know," began Captain Dylan, "in Iraq there have been two Marine Mortuary Affairs units operating. The other MA unit has received their orders to go home. So for the time being we will be the only remaining Marine MA support group in Iraq. We will remain here for the time being, doing other maneuvers.

The best time frame I can give you for our unit to leave Iraq is in mid-to-late September."

Groans cascaded throughout the room as the Captain nodded understanding of their disappointment.

"I do realize this is going to create problems back home for all of us. Families have bills to pay, some Devil Dogs now have little Devil Dogs they haven't even seen yet, and wives and girlfriends are as anxious to be in our arms as we are to be back in theirs. But just so you know you're not alone, my own wedding day will have to be canceled. I too will be hoping my family still loves me when I get home. The only thing I do know for sure is that if this is where I'm going to have to be for the next few months, I'm glad it's with all of you!"

"Hoo-Rah!"

"All right! Now, I'm just as tired as all of you are of staying in some old Republican Guard shit hole like this where they promised us phones and internet access that we're still waiting for," continued Captain Dylan with more than a little anger in his voice. "Higher Command is wanting us to head out and help search all these suspected mass gravesites where Saddam's regime reportedly dumped their dissidents. The good news is, we won't have to do it from here."

"Listen up Marines," the Captain smiled with an upbeat tone, "we are heading for Babylon. If you know anything about Hammurabi, Nebuchadnezzar, the great Hanging Gardens, or the Tower of Babel you'll soon see why this area must be preserved. The Palace of Babylon is located on the banks of the Euphrates River and was built by Saddam Hussein so he could try and somehow tie himself into Babylon's rich history. This is now the official Marine headquarters south of Baghdad. It is where you will sleep with up to one thousand other

Marines, a three star General, and even a chaplain. We'll operate out of a well-fortified and supplied base. You'll also be able to make phone calls and have the Internet. Both systems are up and running."

Loud roars came from the Marines.

"Communication with families will be easier," nodded Captain Dylan, "which will undoubtedly make the time left here go by a little quicker. First Sergeant Ralston, we are to pull out of this shit hole in two days. Do you think we are capable of doing it by tomorrow?"

"Yes Captain Dylan! These damn Devil Dogs are capable of just about anything humanly possible!" roared First Sergeant Ralston. "I do not know about anyone else, but I am in great need of daily Internet access. If these Devil Dogs can't help to quickly satisfy my need on their own, then maybe my big boot kicking some ass will have to help spur their mobility?"

"HOO-RAH!"

*   *   *

When the company of Marines was ready to pull out of Al Kut, Mark had a surprise as he walked toward the lead vehicle and saw Angelo happily ensconced up in the machine gun turret.

"Angelo, get the hell out of there!"

"No, he's fine," Captain Dylan informed him as he walked up. "I'd actually like you to drive for a while, Sebastian. Major combat operations are over so let him get his kicks. His constant chatter was starting to drive me a little crazy anyway."

"I know exactly what you mean," nodded Mark.

"I'm sure you do. Good to go? Then let's roll!"

The two Marines got into their vehicle and led the convoy as it left Al Kut heading south.

"The best roads will take us back down toward Diwaniya, then north through Al Hilla to Karbala," explained the Captain. "We're going to have to pass through the same area where we got ambushed. Are you going to be alright with that?"

"I'm cool with it, Captain. It's not really hot around there any more, is it?"

"We hope not, but who really knows any more?" shrugged Captain Dylan. "In some villages the Iraqis didn't even seem to know we were coming in the first place, so news of the war being over may not have reached everywhere yet."

"I don't have a problem with what happened in that village," Mark assured him. "I'd do the same thing all over again if I had to. Quicker if I could."

"Now that's what I like to hear," nodded Captain Dylan as the convoy rolled down the highway. "Take the next right. You and Angelo remind me a lot of what I was like during the Gulf War in '91. I was your age, just a Corporal. After I got out I went to college, got my degree and then re-enlisted to become an officer. My family thought I was totally insane, but I'm where I want to be right now and unlike a lot of officers I like to think I know what you're going through right now."

"You do seem to be really tuned in to us," observed Mark as he negotiated a right turn onto a narrow paved road. "What I'm wondering is how you managed to put up with Angelo this long? He drives me nuts after a few minutes. He can't hear us, can he?"

"In a noisy military Humvee over these lousy roads did you ever hear us talking about you? I didn't think so," smiled the Captain. "Don't worry, none of it was bad. Private First Class Cicci is one of your biggest supporters. Marines are tough ass killers but the ones who exhibit true character are the ones who inspire others to greatness. That's what it's all about. A few good men, then a few more who rise above the rest."

"I'm not any better than anyone else, Captain."

"Time will tell. Time will tell..."

"Hey, quit talking shit about me, Shark!" yelled down Angelo from the gun turret.

* * *

Hearing the cell phone ring, Dante cleaned the shampoo off his head and leaned out of the shower.

"Hello..."

"Dad!"

"Mark!"

"We've moved to Babylon, at the palace here, which is cool," said Mark from the phone trailer outside the massive palace on a pleasant evening in Iraq.

"Babylon? Why did they move you there?"

"We're the only Marine support group left in Iraq doing what we do. The bad news is we probably won't be coming home until September."

"*September?*" Dante angrily shut off the water and grabbed a towel while stepping out. "I don't understand, the war is supposed to be over now."

"We just do what we're told. You'd have to ask someone higher up."

"Believe me, I'd like to!"

"Try not to get too upset, Dad. If we have to be in Iraq, Babylon is a good safe place to be."

"If you say so."

"Hey, it's really like a vacation after all we went through to get here. What's going on at home?"

"It's starting to get pretty hot so Stephanie and I went hiking out at Red Rock Canyon while the weather is still reasonable."

"Every day here that it doesn't hit a hundred and ten degrees is now reasonable to us. Tell Dudley thanks for sending me all of the CIA stuff. You haven't fired him yet, have you?"

"I actually promoted him in a weak moment. Are you serious about culinary school?"

"Don't know, Dad. I'm just serious about having some options other than being a Marine all my life."

"Well, just let me know if I can be of any help."

"Don't worry, I will. Listen Dad, I have to go. Angelo is holding my place in the email line so I'll hit up your message box with more as soon as I can."

"At the hotel or here at the house?"

"Both, we're back to the future now!"

"Well, it's about time…"

* * *

MARK'S JOURNAL:

We've been here in Babylon for just over a week now, camped with a thousand other Marines plus tanks and artillery units at the base of a huge palace built by Saddam on the banks of the Euphrates River. At night we get to go up to the palace and sleep inside, which is so much better than being in a tent outside. The palace was looted extensively by the locals before Marines moved in and there aren't any fixtures or windows left, but you can tell it was pretty ornate once. To one side of the palace are the old ruins, the Tower of Babel, the Hanging Gardens, and all that jazz. We haven't had time to go looking around yet, but the Captain has promised to take us all on a field trip through the ruins sometime soon.

On the way over to our new home it was like the Yogi Berra saying about it *being deja vu all over again* when we drove through the town where we were ambushed before. Evidently, there had been more trouble after we left the first time and a couple of helicopter gunships had torn up the whole town pretty good. It was basically in ruins when we passed through, and we didn't see a single head pop out while we drove through, which is good considering Angelo would have unloaded every last round at the first hint of trouble.

I did feel just a little strange going through there again, but it wasn't like I was afraid that something might happen, or had a guilt trip about what really did happen. I just remembered how fast it all unfolded. We react to aggression with instinct developed by our training. That's what they teach us and it works. I looked out to find the little house I'd fired on but there wasn't anything left. It had been reduced to rubble. Just as well. What happened there was buried in the past.

The very first day after we got to Babylon we had to go back to Hilla, which is only just a few clicks away down the road. A Marine had died when he stepped on a piece of unexploded ordnance, maybe one of our cluster bomb-lets that didn't go off when it first hit the ground. It was a grim reminder to everyone to not let their guard down and to be very careful at all times. The next day there was an explosion in one of our own munitions bunkers near the palace from a fire and another Marine lost his life.

I've been phoning and e-mailing everyone as much as I can. It feels good to talk to people every other day or so and catch up on stuff. Plus we're getting news of the world as it happens now instead of hearing about things a few weeks or a month after the fact. I guess this is good, but there are some things I don't really like to hear about, like how the Iraqis are starting to resist our efforts. They should be thanking us for liberating them, but I guess some of them are angry that we haven't turned the country back over to them yet.

But we can't do that until there's solid proof Saddam and all his closest people are dead and no longer a threat. Those of us who are serving over here wish the process was going faster too, but I guess reality is turning out to be a bitch. We've heard there's a lot of fighting over in Fallujah between the Army and locals, which really isn't surprising since it is part of the Sunni Triangle stronghold in western Iraq.

We heard there was a big terrorist bombing in Saudi Arabia and two more in Israel, so I guess these terrorists just aren't going to go down without a fight. But they will go down, for sure, sooner or later.

Yesterday Angelo was talking to one of his brothers and he told Angelo that the guy we initially sent over to Iraq to administer reconstruction had been fired and replaced by this new guy. First thing he did was lay off 400,000 Iraqi soldiers who we thought were going to be re-trained to police their country so all the Marines and Army soldiers could go home sooner. But I guess not, even if it doesn't seem to make much sense. It's their country and they should police it, not us.

Some commentators on television claim this is like instantly creating 400,000 enemies for us over here. Guys are starting to worry a little about what's happening because some locals are still shooting at us, mostly at night when we know better than to go out on the roads unless we absolutely have to.

We're starting to get reports about IED's, or Improvised Explosive Devices. These are roadside bombs being detonated either by contact with one of our vehicles, or by handheld remote controls. This is definitely bad news for Marines and the Army since it is hard to detect where they might be. Where we are staying now is pretty safe, but anything can happen so we still have to be just as alert as we ever were before.

I wrote the above this morning when I woke up, but then we had an emergency and the whole convoy headed out again. I drove us to the Shatt Al Hilla Canal where a CH-46 Sea Knight helicopter (like the one which crashed in Kuwait the first night of the war) had gone down into the canal. We don't know if it was from a mechanical problem or a rocket hit.

We were out there all day and it was a pretty bad scene. Four Marines on the helicopter died in the crash. To make matters worse, one of the rescuers who got to the scene first drowned while trying to save them. We were guarding the perimeter while they pulled the wreckage and bodies out and I know it had to tear a lot of guys up. No one said much on the ride back to camp. It's something you hope you can forget, but you know you'll probably never be able to.

*   *   *

EMAIL:
To: Emmy
From: Mark

Hey Em, I tried to phone but all I keep getting is your answering machine. You haven't been home much so I started thinking you'd met that special someone. Then I realized it was Memorial Day weekend and you were probably flying around the country going crazy.

Overall, things are pretty much okay here. Since we're assigned to Mortuary Affairs we've been busy working at a site near Al Hilla where we found massive graves where all these people who opposed the former regime were executed, then dumped into a big ditch and bulldozed over. It's been pretty gross but it needs to be done. Another reason why coming here to Iraq was necessary. If it was thought you ever opposed Saddam Hussein in the least you'd wind up dead and buried in a hole with hundreds of others. At least no one was shooting at us while we were excavating remains.

Grandpa's birthday is coming up and obviously I won't be there. Dad is flying out to Sacramento for the party. Will you be going too? If you do, please pick up a present for me? I know Grandpa doesn't really need too much except a new heart and a memory stick, but I want him to know I'm thinking about him since I can't call where he is now. I'll pay for whatever you pick up.

Mom is pissed off that it's going to take so long for me to come home. I'm sure she's already expressed those feelings to you. I'm not exactly happy about the timeline we're stuck with either, but try and convince her not to waste a lot of time calling her Congressman. I don't think it'll do much good.

We only have about fifteen weeks left here so we're hoping to do our time fast and safely. We're all just glad we don't have to stay here for a whole year like some Army guys and gals will have to. Having to be here during the holidays would be really depressing.

Anyway, I'll try calling you next week.

Love, Mark

June 2003

A profusely sweating Angelo stood sheepishly in the palace command office while an extremely angry Captain Dylan circled like a vulture eyeing rotten meat.

"Private First Class Cicci, I shit you not! If you ever pull a stunt like this again, I will personally bust your ass down so far and so fast your head will be spinning like that little girl in the Exorcist. You will be out of this unit and stuck in Iraq for a full year cleaning latrines or hopefully worse. Now do you understand the words which are coming out of my mouth?"

"Yes Captain, I'm sorry," nodded Angelo very timidly. "I don't know what I was thinking."

"You obviously weren't thinking of any of your fellow Marines who could've gotten killed!"

"I just reacted to what was happening. Guess I probably shouldn't have."

"Damn right you shouldn't have!" agreed the Captain, barking into Angelo's ear. "You interfered with another Marine unit and not only put your friends in great danger but the other unit too. Maybe I should send you down the hall to the General and let him tell you what he thinks about your decision making prowess?"

"I think I can imagine what he'd say, Captain."

"What the hell is the problem with you, Cicci?" wondered Captain Dylan. "Are you so hardheaded you just forget your orders and training at the drop of a hat? What you did was selfish and stupid. It was also one of the bravest and noblest things a man could ever do. But do us all a big favor and save the heroics for your own time! While you are here in Iraq, either do it the Marine way or not at all. Now get the hell out of my sight!"

Angelo saluted and hurried out, scurrying down the stairs dragging his tail between his legs after the loud tongue-lashing. It was readily evident most of the Marines on the bottom floor of the palace had heard Captain Dylan's loud tirade. Some frowned angrily, others snickered at him, and there were those who were laughing at his sad plight. Two of them were Sykes and Valdespino, who escorted Angelo out of the palace.

"How does it feel to be a hero, Angelo?" asked Valdespino, enjoying the Italian's discomfort.

"A hero who just got another asshole reamed for him by the Captain," added Sykes.

"Screw you guys! Is Shark still pissed at me?"

"What would he be mad about, that you almost got us all killed while we were out buying chickens?"

"The only reason we're able to laugh is because we couldn't possibly be as mad at you as Shark is," explained Valdespino. "It'll be a pleasure watching him kick your sorry little meatball ass from one end of Babylon to the other. You're about to become part of the ruins. Angelo hanging by his balls from the gardens of Babylon. Hey, I kind of like the sound of it."

"I'd better give Shark more time to cool off," decided Angelo. "Let's go get some lunch."

"Thanks to you we won't be eating any chicken, that's for damn sure," noted Sykes.

*   *   *

Dante hurried into the house still dressed in his golf clothes. He left his bag in the front hall, checked the kitchen clock, and hurried into the family room to turn on the television set where Diana Scott appeared on the screen to stare back at him.

"Welcome back to 'Three Voices'. With the Iraq reconstruction process facing new difficulties and insurgent actions against American troops experiencing an alarming increase, we have much to discuss."

The men nodded back to her while eyeing each other with varying degrees of contempt.

"The bottom line is we did the right thing in Iraq and the Iraqi people are grateful we did so," offered General Pynchon. "We are making solid progress in bringing an interim provisional government to Iraq so their people will be able to govern themselves for the first time in almost a quarter century. We are restoring Iraq's infrastructure and providing internal security so schools, public services, and commerce can flourish where it couldn't have before. Most importantly, we continue to track down the remaining remnants of Saddam Hussein's regime and are getting closer every day to finding their weapons of mass destruction."

"Fitz, you sound like you're becoming one of those people who think if they say weapons of mass destruction enough times they'll somehow just magically appear one day," observed Congressman Ballantree, shaking his head sadly. "We've been in Iraq over three months now, and have had unabated access to any location where any of this contraband might be. We haven't found anything yet, and we never will."

"Unless the United States actually plants some evidence there, I am very confident it will never exist," agreed the Arab journalist.

"I look forward to the day when you're both eating more crow than you're used to, if that's possible" spoke General Pynchon. "I've got Doubting Thomas on one side here and Paranoid Mohammed on the other."

"Gentlemen, let's put all of that to rest now," suggested Diana Scott, "and deal with the post-war reconstruction in Iraq. What is happening now, what has gone wrong, and what needs to improve? Recently the Deputy Defense Secretary appeared before the Senate Foreign Relations Committee and characterized the situation as improving but still difficult, if not downright messy. In response, Senators criticized the administration for drafting a detailed plan for removing Saddam Hussein from power, but failing to put together a similar strategy for stabilizing and rebuilding Iraq. Your reaction, Congressman?"

"It's not a question of whether the post-war plan has gone wrong," Congressman Ballantree pointed out. "It's a matter of if you can even determine there was a cognitive plan to begin with in the first place. If your thinking is wishful or initially just plain skewered, and you conceive some jumble of a direction that is going to be impossible to execute, how can you even insert these results and the word strategy into the same sentence?"

"That's a complete crock Wayne, and you know it!" thundered the General. "Armchair quarterbacking from alarmists like you is entirely responsible for not helping the situation or our troop morale with all these wildly inaccurate portrayals of the real truth. All of this negative propaganda is the work of a decidedly biased liberal press, obvious partisan politics, and some very clear anti-American interests."

"Meaning people like me, General?" asked Al Khayyam. "Miss Scott, the answer to your query has its roots in the original basis for beginning this war in the first place. Those reasons were tenuous at best, and at the worst a great lie. The war is won and again we have the reasons for reconstruction, which are tenuous at best and at the worst a great lie. In any event the reason for war was not as it seemed, nor was this veil to hide a conquest and occupation disguised as noble and just."

"Just another obvious example of the truncated conspiracy theories he's so famous for editorializing on," concluded General Pynchon with firm conviction. "That's right, I've been reading some of the garbage you are spewing out and I'm surprised to see you even showing your face out in public after delivering some of it. Anyone who believes something as preposterous as this nonsense and debates it in a public forum doesn't even deserve the dignity of a response. The situation is certainly chaotic right now, but there are a lot of situations you simply can't plan for, like having a population repressed for so long that when they are finally presented with the freedom to bring about democratic change, they don't know what the hell to do with it. Worse yet, they won't trust the only people who can teach them how to do it. Now, is that our fault?"

"It certainly is!" nodded the Congressman. "We should have been able to predict this cause and effect so there was an actual strategy to deal with this and every other contingency. That's what good planning on any level is all about. Now, if the administration had come to Congress before the war and told us the real truth about the reconstruction of Iraq after war being a lot more expensive, being fraught with peril, and perhaps even becoming an unmanageable situation, I can guarantee you even most Republicans would not have voted to support this war in any way, shape, or form."

"Hide the real truth until it's too late to stop it." .

"Horse feathers!" lamented the General loudly. "Neither one of you knows what the hell you're talking about! Miss Scott, please have someone get me an antacid? These morons are turning my stomach."

"If you cannot catch Saddam or keep his loyalists from planning insurgent attacks against your troops, and if you don't have an honest plan to stabilize

Iraq internally and still conform to the needs of Iraq's powerful clerics," proposed Al Khayyam, "then you may have won the battle but inevitably you'll wind up losing the real war, and thus not dignifying all the sacrifices made by the young men and women of your military and their families. In any country, this can only result in political suicide for the ruling party."

"Thank you, Gentlemen. That's all we have time for today. This is Diana Scott and we'll be back with more of 'Three Voices' next week. Good-bye…"

* * *

The assisted living center was located in the woody, rolling hills north of Sacramento off the highway leading to Lake Tahoe. In the private patio outside Grandpa Marcus Sebastian's spacious bungalow were gathered sons Ray and Dante, Ray's wife Jeannie, Dante's friend Stephanie and daughter Emmy. Grandpa Marcus' private nurse Flo was never too far away to see to the eighty year old patriarch's every want and need. A birthday cake was prominently displayed on a table.

The smiling old ex-Marine was clearly pleased to have so many of his loved ones around him while he sat in his wheelchair. The adults were all drinking wine, even Marcus. Emmy stood next to his chair, one arm draped around his shoulder.

"Good to have you all here," Grandpa Marcus began. "I'm sorry my own Emily couldn't make it, but she went ahead of me to do a little scouting last year."

"Mom died two years ago, Dad," corrected Ray.

"Was it really that long ago?" frowned Marcus in surprise. "Then what the hell am I still doing here?"

"Watching over us," said Emmy with a hug.

"And a big damn job that is!" Marcus chuckled. "Say, where's my buddy boy? What's his name?"

"Mark."

"Right, Mark! You named him after me, Ray?"

"My Dad is his father," corrected Emmy. "Mark was named after you, like I was named after Grandma."

"That makes sense. Well, where is that boy?" Grandpa wanted to know, looking around.

Emmy leaned down to Marcus's eye level.

"He's over in Iraq, Grandpa."

"Iraq? What the hell is he doing over there?"

"He's in the Marines, remember Dad?" offered Ray. "You saw him in his uniform last Thanksgiving."

"That was Thanksgiving?" frowned Marcus. "I thought it was Halloween? Who let him go over there?"

"When he turned eighteen, it was his decision," explained Dante. "We didn't know he enlisted."

"But he's just a kid and those damn people over there are crazier than even I am," suggested Marcus.

"The war is over, Dad," Ray assured him.

"Yes, I know it's over!" snapped back his father. "I'm just old, not stupid. What do you think I watch on my television all day, cartoons? Well why isn't he home yet? Marines go, fight, win, and come home again. What the hell are they doing over there now?"

"Peacekeeping, it seems," Emmy informed him.

"Peacekeeping? Marines aren' good at that!"

"Grandpa, Mark will be home soon," Emmy assured him. "He asked me to give you this present. Want me to open it for you?"

"Go ahead. I'm practically all thumbs now," he said in childish anticipation.

Emmy unwrapped a picture and showed it to him. A group of Marines were pulling down a statue of

Saddam Hussein with their vehicles in downtown Baghdad as Iraqis cheered.

"Now this is what I'm talking about!" beamed the old man while squinting his eyes to look over the picture in detail. "Which one is my buddy boy?"

"Well he's not actually in the picture," explained Emmy. "It's more symbolic than anything else. I'm sure Mark was doing something else important at the time."

"Well if anything happens to him, whoever's responsible will have me to deal with," warned Marcus. "After I die I hope to be reincarnated as a bird, and I will make it a point to fly over everyone who might be even remotely responsible for anything going wrong with anyone in my family, and take a big dump on them every day for the rest of their miserable lives."

Shrieks of laughter filled the patio. Grandpa's nurse came over to make sure he was okay.

"Now don't get too excited, Marcus!"

"Then you better not get too close, Flo," Marcus replied. "You know what you do to me…"

"Grandpa, she's your nurse!"

"Oh, she's a lot more than that," intimated Marcu, looking up to his smiling fifty-year-old nurse with puppy dog eyes. "I'll admit she's my fantasy girl."

Flo was embarrassed, trying to explain.

"Marcus is very charming and loves to flirt. But ours is an affair of the imagination only."

"That can be pretty wicked in itself, Flo,"

"Whatever makes you happy, Marcus. Just call if you need me," Flo smiled, leaving them after giving Marcus a pat on the shoulder.

"When my dear Emily left me," Marcus started to explain after Flo disappeared, "all the fun seemed to go out of my life. We flirted with each other every day we were together because we knew it would keep our hearts and minds young even when our bodies grew old. Love and laughter make life worth living no matter what else happens."

"Do you think Mom would approve of Flo?"

"I think so, Dante. I like to think there's more than a little bit of my Emily in her, and I'll tell you why," Grandpa Marcus smiled with sparkling eyes. "I never flirted with a woman in my life after I met your mother. She had big ears, big eyes, and most importantly a big mind. If I'd even think something about another woman she could read me like a dime novel. Come to think of it, she had a big nose too."

"Grandpa!"

"Anyway," continued the family patriarch, "One day not long after my Emily was gone I was sitting right here feeling sorry for myself. Every time I close my eyes I can still see her looking at me the way she always looked at all of us she loved. Flo had just been assigned to me a few weeks before and was a real hard ass to begin with. So when she found me out here with my eyes closed talking to the love of my life I'm sure she was probably figuring it was onset Alzheimer's."

"But I remember the wind coming up as she was rolling me back inside and I looked back over my shoulder and saw Flo just eating up that wind with her eyes closed and a big smile on her face. I do believe my Emily's spirit had to be in that wind because ever since then Flo's been treating me the same way my Emily would have if she were still here. In a way, it helps me believe she's still here, in the breeze, or maybe just in a smile. Does this make any sense to anyone but me?"

The patio was silent, very touched by his words.

"My Emily always used to say *whatever makes you happy*. The funny thing is, I don't remember ever telling Flo about what Emily used to say, but now she says it to me too, all the time."

The patio was completely quiet in thought. Some were stunned while others had a knowing smile. Grandpa Marcus was delighted he'd got to them all. His eyes moved around the patio, found Dante's smiling eyes, then turned to the woman beside him. He appeared to close his eyes as if drifting off, then opened them and winked at her with sparkling eyes.

"Hey there, pretty lady."

"Hello, Marcus," Stephanie smiled back at him.

"You're very young. Did my son adopt you?"

"He hasn't proposed anything like that yet."

"Well, if you really do like older men," hinted Marcus, "Flo and I really aren't exactly going steady."

"Yes you are! Don't tease me, Marcus."

"Oh, I like this one, Dante!" nodded Marcus to his son. "Why haven't you married her yet?"

"Dad, we've only been dating awhile."

"Who knows how long any of us really have? Don't waste time," he counseled. "Do you love her?"

"Dad, please…"

"It's a simple question," pressed Marcus. "Do you, or do you not love her?"

Dante was embarrassed as he found his family, including a smiling Emmy, looking on expectantly. He looked into Stephanie's eyes briefly and then answered.

"Absolutely."

"Now, is that absolutely yes, or absolutely no?" clarified Grandpa Marcus, enjoying himself immensely.

"Yes, definitely yes."

Dante and Stephanie kissed softly while the rest of the family clapped and cheered. Grandpa Marcus smiled proudly at Stephanie and gave her a big thumbs up. She winked back at him with a happy tear.

"Now who is going to cut that fine cake? As you can all see I'm crying for a piece…"

* * *

"Remember that Beatles song?" asked Angelo as the four soldiers ate dinner in the mess tent. *"When I get older, losing my hair, many years from now…"*

"Hey, I know that song," nodded Sykes. "Can't seem to remember the name of it though…"

"Well before my time," claimed Mark.

"What do you guys think we'll all be like when we're old?" continued Angelo.

"First Sergeant Ralston will probably be like the Great Black Santini," Mark predicted.

"Captain Dylan will be Colonel, maybe higher," nodded Valdespino confidently.

"I see Wichita sitting around in a rocking chair on his farm smoking a corn cob pipe," offered Angelo, "scratching his ass, swigging a jug of moonshine, and talking to a bunch of animals and rugrats."

"Sounds good to me if it means I'll be alive."

"I can see Larry in a panama hat smoking Cuban cigars while driving all his grandchildren around South Beach in some low rider convertible tapping one of his tunes on the steering wheel."

"I could live with that," smiled Valdespino.

"Shark will wind up a chef like his father, only just not as good. He'll spend a good deal of his free time staring off into space wondering why he couldn't ever land a hot young babe like I did."

"Whatever!" laughed Mark with the others. "What about you, Angelo? Professional wrestling? Or maybe something even more fake, like politics?"

"Mayor Cicci, Senator Cicci, Alderman Cicci, Chief of Police Cicci," sounded off Angelo. "They all have a nice ring to them. It will be hard to decide!"

"I think Angelo is going to wind up an inmate because of some scam he thinks up," suggested Sykes.

"Maybe so, but I'll run that freaking prison."

"I can see you," said Valdespino with his eyes closed, visualizing it, "as this fat, balding, belching, farting, wine guzzling Italian who is sitting around wondering why all his kids seem to be turning out to be just as disappointing, dishonest, and distrustful as him."

"I could do that, Larry," agreed Angelo. "In fact, that's what most of my family does now anyway. We like having a lot of shit to bitch about to other people. Of course, I could still be mayor at the same time."

*　　*　　*

"The Marine who just died in his tent," ventured Mark as he drove the Captain away from a Marine base. "Was it classified as a non-combative gunshot wound?"

"Yes. That's the third one in two weeks."

"Non-combative means when a gun kills you it's either a mistake while cleaning it, or it's self-inflicted. I don't understand why a Marine would commit suicide?"

"Wish we had the answer but afraid we don't," sighed Captain Dylan. "We are trained to recognize the early warning signs so there can be intervention when someone becomes overly depressed or is clearly in emotional trouble. But some guys keep it all inside until whatever it is just eats them up. Loneliness, anxiety, relationship problems at home, fear of the unexpected, traumatic experiences on the battlefield, who really knows what can damage someone's soul so deeply that they're willing to end their own life? Some leave notes or mail home first, while others don't leave any reason as to why they did it. It's not much consolation but the Army is having a much bigger problem than we are.

"I'm glad we won't still be here during the holidays. It will just get worse then."

"Roger on that, Sebastian."

July 2003

Outside the palace in the hot sun a makeshift fighting ring was surrounded by boisterous off-duty Marines and no one was enjoying the spectacle more than Sykes and Valdespino.

"Happy Fourth of July to sports fans all over the world! Welcome to the Palace of Babylon in Iraq where we continue our exclusive coverage of the first ever Marine Independence Day Olympics featuring some of the greatest Marine athletes in the world," announced Sykes into an empty soda can. "This is the one and only 'Wichita Tornado' Jimmy Sykes and we are here for the final event of the day, the much anticipated Mixed Martial Arts championship match. Joining me is my color commentator, 'The South Miami Scorpion' Hilario Valdespino. Welcome to the booth, Larry."

"Thank you, Jimmy," said Valdespino speaking into his own empty soda can as he wedged down onto the ground next to Sykes. "Who would've figured last year one of Saddam's ornate palaces would be serving on America's Independence Day for one of the premier Martial Arts events in the entire world. I don't know about you but I'm very excited to be here."

"Frankly Larry, we're surprised to even have your services available today. When I first glimpsed the draw for this tournament and saw the name of a much-heralded championship high school wrestler like you in it, I immediately penciled you in for the finals despite the obvious height and weight advantage you give up to all your opponents."

"Why thank you very much, Wichita," replied Valdespino as humbly as possible. "As you may well know, I am one of the toughest Devil Dogs operating south of Baghdad but my hopes in this tournament were waylaid earlier in the quarter-finals when I went up against a force I just couldn't reckon with."

"Angelo 'The Mangler' Cicci is a badass."

"Certainly, but even tougher when he cheats!" complained Valdespino. "These are his bite marks on my arm and you saw him knee me in the nuts."

"Yes, but I really wish I hadn't," reported Sykes. "Unfortunately, the referee didn't see it either."

"Do you think I should get a tetanus shot?"

"Without question, and please do it very soon," suggested Sykes. "After beating you, 'The Mangler' is in the finals against an opponent who had a thoroughly difficult test in his own semi-final match."

"Right, Jimmy. Mark 'The Shark' Sebastian met none other than the predictably angry First Sergeant 'Screaming' Oliver Ralston in a bloody match that had this sell-out crowd on its feet. Those two Marines beat the crap out of each other over the ten minute time limit, with a bloody nose suffered by 'The Shark' drenching the crowd in the stuff which makes vampires swoon. But Sebastian got the nod on a split decision, which didn't sit too well with Ralston's camp."

"The match could've gone either way," nodded Sykes. "Ralston is obviously a very mean son of a gun and any Marines who are forced to serve under him should receive some special consideration, like a freaking medal or something. But how much did that match really take out of 'The Shark'? We'll have to see. He's bigger than 'The Mangler' and probably a little stronger, but who do you pick in the finals?"

"This might surprise you Jimmy, but I have to go with 'The Mangler' even though I personally find him to be a very distasteful individual. 'The Shark' is a killer but a good guy and an honest man, while 'The Mangler' is anything but that. One guy will certainly cheat while the other won't, so my money is on the foul-smelling, loud mouthed bad boy from Chicago."

"May I remind you, Larry, that none other than the esteemed Captain Dylan himself will be the referee in this contest. He's done a great job today making sure this competition is not quite brutal enough to put any Marines out of commission for too long, with only one shoulder separation on the injury list. But this is a true clash of the titans. These two men were as close as brothers before the war started, but now there seems to be almost a simmering bitterness between the two, presumably over a mysterious money issue. We can expect blood will be spilled in this match and the *South Miami Scorpion* himself predicts the outcome of this will be determined by an illegal act. Advantage, Cicci!"

"They're coming to the ring right now and the crowd is roaring!" reported Valdespino. 'The Mangler' has dyed his hair blonde! 'The Mangler' has dyed his hair! Where did he find peroxide here in Babylon?"

"It's well known 'The Mangler' has his fingers in everything, even peroxide," revealed Sykes. "Look, 'Screaming' Oliver Ralston is coming out to corner for Angelo. What is up with that? Now here comes 'The Shark' and look at the confident, determined look on his face. That is one tough ass Marine. But he's coming out alone, without a corner man."

"That's not right, Jimmy!" protested Valdespino, quickly rising to his feet. "I'm sorry, but I just can't let this happen. As much as I'd like to be part of this broadcast I am compelled to go support 'The Shark'."

"You've heard it, fans," screamed Sykes over the roar of the crowd. "'The South Beach Scorpion' Hilario Valdespino has left our broadcast booth to go up and support a warrior he isn't even picking to win this fight. We'll be right back with this historic match just as soon as I go and relieve myself..."

*   *   *

MARK'S JOURNAL:

A couple of days ago we got a call from just outside Karbala where a Marine died during a mine clearing operation. It's still never easy to see what happens when one of your brothers is blown up into little pieces. We've been warned about the growing possibility of roadside bombs since what they're now calling an insurgency seems to be getting worse the longer we stay.

The Fourth of July was a blast. There were a lot of events during our Olympics and we were able to forget about everything else for a day. Initially there was just going to be a martial arts points event but some guy got two pairs of MMA gloves sent to him from home so the brass said we could do it instead as long as we didn't hit each other in the head or do anything else to seriously injure someone. I had four fights in less than four hours and the one against First Sergeant Ralston took a lot out of me. He dumped me on my face and my nose wouldn't stop bleeding. I thought I hurt him too since he was covered in blood, but it turned out it was all mine. It went to a decision after ten minutes and I was surprised they gave it to me. The First Sergeant was a pretty good sport about it but I could tell he was still pissed off.

Everyone in our company thought it was pretty cool that two of our guys made it into the finals. Marines like bragging rights and our company really couldn't lose no matter who won. I was beat up and didn't even want to fight, but there's no way I could default to Angelo with all the trash talk he was spouting. He hit me on the side of the head with a punch early on and got warned by the Captain. After that I took him to the ground since he's probably a little better stand-up fighter than I am. I got gassed quickly and he almost made me tap from a chicken wing, but I got out of it and then about five minutes into the match my famous *kimura* arm lock was there so I sunk it in and 'The Mangler' was forced to tap out after just a few seconds of seemingly intense pain.

It felt good to win under the circumstances. I bet a little on myself so it worked out okay. Valdespino and Sykes were happy for me but disappointed since they'd bet on Angelo. 'The Mangler' was actually quite gracious in defeat, more so than I would've imagined.

Later I learned Angelo was actually the big winner since he had bet on me too. A lot. No wonder I was able to get out of the chicken wing. He knew he could lose to me, but wasn't quite sure if he could beat me, so he bet on a sure thing and took a dive while making it look good. 'The Mangler' should really go into pro wrestling. But that blonde hair really has to go.

* * *

Angelo was reading a magazine while they all sat around having breakfast in the mess tent. His hair had been magically transformed back to its natural shade.

"A recent poll says Americans think we are losing control of the situation here."

"Great news, thanks," sighed Mark.

"But the Administration claims it's *improving*."

"Isn't that what they claim every other week?"

"Careful, Wichita! You heard what happened to soldiers who criticized the White House in front of the press," cautioned Valdespino, looking around to see if anyone else was listening.

"Here's a news flash," continued Angelo. "The Jessica Lynch story is officially a hoax! They claimed she was fighting for her life during that ambush, shooting Iraqis and shit. Turns out she was unconscious after her truck crashed and her rifle was jammed."

"At least she got home alive. All that matters."

"Why do they claim this shit?"

"I don't understand it either," agreed Mark.

"Just plain ass embarrassing," noted Sykes.

"Here's another news flash: There is a twenty five million dollar reward for the capture of Saddam, but for some reason it doesn't apply to any of us."

"Money just slips through your hands, Angelo."

"No thanks to you, Shark," replied Angelo. "Here is some good news. Both of Saddam Hussein's sons were killed *in a blaze of gunfire and rockets*."

"Too bad we missed the party," lamented Sykes.

"Listen to this shit," continued Angelo, trying to control his laughter. "The President was flying on Air Force One talking to the press and actually admitted he isn't very analytical, and doesn't spend a lot of time thinking about himself or why he does things."

"Our Commander-in-Chief?"

"Well, it does make sense when you think about it," thought Sykes. "Maybe it's why he made that *Bring 'em on* speech ? Obviously, he wasn't *thinking*."

"No shit! One of the Army guys I know says the rebels or insurgents or whoever the hell they are have been *bringing it on* ever since then," related Angelo. "The Army is losing like two or three guys every day. I guess maybe that's what happens when the people in charge don't think about what they're doing or saying. Things start to go wrong for you, real quick."

"I remember my Dad telling me the same thing when I was young," offered Mark, yawning. "At least I learned my lesson. I sure wish some of the so-called adults in Washington would do so too."

*   *   *

MARK'S JOURNAL:

Sometimes in the business we are in, we don't have to go very far to find work. It was early in the morning and an alarm sounded in camp. The defense perimeter was re-enforced and we all hurried over to join a bunch of other Marines at the back of the palace.

A Marine was down on the ground dead. At first we thought it might be a sniper but it was soon determined he'd fallen to his death from a guard post about sixty feet up on the palace wall. I recognized him from around the camp. I can even remember seeing him smiling and joking around with his buddies in the mess hall just a few days before. You just never know what's going to happen here, or when.

We've been hearing more shots fired from the direction of Karbala. Two days after the Marine died in our camp another Marine lost his life in a non-hostile gunshot wound not far from here. There's been a change in the air around here, and not for the better.

August 2003

MARK'S JOURNAL:

From what I've been able to learn about this country I've been, the land we now know as Iraq has always been at war. Saddam Hussein tried to liken himself to be a modern day hero like say Hammurabi or Nebuchadnezzar, but there is no parallel.

How will history look at this war we're currently in? Will it be seen as an occupation as the Iraqi people and the Arab world seem to think it is, or as an act of liberation like Washington wants everyone else to believe? Or is this entire story just going to be a footnote to something else bigger which happens somewhere else down the road? History can be fascinating if you really care about it enough. Actually though, I don't really care about this country or its people very much any more, or how history portrays what we're doing over here right now. All I want to do right now is to just go home alive.

The rest is just history.

*   *   *

From the palace phone Mark called his sister.
She turned on a light at three in the morning.
"Hello…"
"Hey Emmy…"
"Mark! Is everything okay?"
"I don't know…"
"It sounds like you're kind of down?"

"I guess. Just needed to hear your voice."

"It's fine, don't worry," she assured him.

"We only have six weeks left here, and when you really want to leave somewhere it almost seems like time stands still," he tried to explain. "Hours seem like days, days like weeks, and weeks like months. The sand fleas keep eating us up every other second, and everyone here is really on edge right now."

"I know how you must feel," she commiserated. "I've felt the same way since January and the closer it gets to you coming home the longer it seems to be. Just stay positive and don't lose your sense of humor. Make plans to do all the things you want to do when you get back. Keep your mind busy and time will fly by."

"I'll try. How are the parents doing?"

"Well, I hate to tell you this, but Mom is already planning a series of West Palm Beach *soirees* for when you get back. I guess she's been lining up some suitable young debutantes for you to meet and hopefully marry. But she did mention something about finding a little fixer-upper for your friend and his wife in Miami."

"Good news on the latter, but I'm not looking for any help on the former," replied Mark. "Mom's really going to be pissed when I don't show up for most of what she's planning, but the last thing I want to do when I get back is have a bunch of strangers asking me about what I did over here and what I want to do next."

"I can imagine. It's your birthday next week!"

"I can hardly wait," he said facetiously. "I'll be legally old enough to buy my first drink and I'm in a country where you can't legally buy any alcohol. Something is definitely wrong with this picture."

"Make up for it when you get back."

"Any news from Dad he hasn't told me?"

"From what I understand through my network of spies," reported Emmy confidentially, "one of whom works at Tiffany's on the Strip, a certain well-known local chef was seen enthusiastically shopping for an engagement ring with a very attractive and definitely younger female hotel executive."

"Whoa! This is getting serious."

"Looks like it."

"He does seem to be a lot happier now."

"True. Grandpa likes her so she must be okay."

"I want to go see Grandpa when I get back."

"He's counting the days. Is it still really hot?"

"No, it's down to only about one ten or so. Our officers keep ragging on us every day about getting lots of fluids and eating properly. Still, we've heard some soldiers have died from the heat. I actually traded jobs with Angelo a while ago and he's been begging to change back because of the heat and dust, but I kind of like where I'm at now. Captain Dylan is a cool dude to ride with and I get to hear more about what's going on."

"One ten? That's Vegas weather, handle it."

"Not the heat that's bothering me. It's the fleas."

"You be careful now, Mark. You'll be home soon and there aren't many sand fleas here."

"Deal. I'll trade Nevada scorpions for Iraqi fleas any day. We're having some drills in a few minutes so I have to get back to my unit. I'll call again soon."

"I love you, Mark. Thanks for thinking of me."

"Always. I love you too, Emmy."

*   *   *

Continuing toward his tent one fine morning, Mark spied Angelo emerging from the latrines. Angelo ran to catch up with his friend.

"Shark…"

"Angelo…Why all the mail. Most people don't want to sit in a smelly latrine reading their mail."

"Poppa met your Dad at a convention in Vegas."

"Heard. What is a funeral home convention?"

"They make speeches about the industry and talk about ways to increase business without actually going out and killing people, marketing stuff mostly. Then they have a trade show which is like a car show for caskets and hearses and urns. Plus you can find out about the latest embalming equipment and methods, and if you need a new crematory oven, Las Vegas will be the best place to get a really good deal."

"Sounds very exciting."

"If you only knew. I got dragged along to a few of them, kicking and screaming all the way. People in the funeral business are known to be a little stiff and formal since it's by nature a very solemn business. But when the show closes for the day, the guys in black suits know how to get down and dirty. Strip clubs know business will be good when there's a funeral operator convention in town. Think about having to spend all of your days surrounded by dead bodies and mourners, and then suddenly you're presented with the golden opportunity to be around some live, nude, gyrating ass action. Then heaven gains a whole new meaning. "

"I see a new batch of magazines. What news do you have from the world?"

"Arnold is running for Governor of California."

"Yeah, right…"

"I'm not shitting you, he really is. They're having a recall election because the present Governor screwed up the state's finances pretty badly so Arnold announced he was running on Jay Leno's show."

"Wasn't he born in Austria or another planet?"

"I think so," replied Angelo, "but apparently the only rule is you can't run for President if you were born in a foreign country. I guess it's alright if you just want to be some freaking Governor."

"Do you think he really has a chance to win?"

"He's already leading at the polls. Go figure..."

"If he gets elected he might just terminate everyone?" suggested Mark in a bad Austrian accent.

"That's what I'm thinking too. Now for more bad news, foreign peacekeeping troops are going to start arriving here in the next few weeks. But despite intense lobbying from Washington to get us more help, foreign countries are only committing about half the troops we asked for, which means there won't be enough foreign soldiers to replace our troops here, which means we can't withdraw most of them from Iraq until early next year. Now, this doesn't affect our present deployment since we're going home soon, but it doesn't mean they can't still send us back over here."

"Sometimes I wish we'd get less news. How about the actual war here?"

"Seriously? You're ready to hear the truth?"

"No," sighed Mark, "but tell me anyway."

"Okay, more troops have now actually died in Iraq after the President declared major combat operations were over, than died during the main coalition invasion, which means the Army is getting hit a hell of a lot harder than we are. Iraqi insurgents are now targeting Iraqi police and anyone else cooperating with the United States. Suicide bombers from foreign countries are flooding over the border from other Muslim countries to join the insurgency fighting occupying forces, meaning us. The consensus is we are still at war and peace is nowhere near at hand."

"I just don't get it," questioned Mark, confused. "How could we start out so well here and now have it going badly so damn fast?"

"The way I see it Shark," proposed Angelo in a philosophical light, "is in reality it all comes down to having the wrong ingredients."

"What do you mean?"

"Well, your Dad is a chef so let me lay it out for you in the sort of culinary terms you might understand," suggested Angelo. "Okay, we started out with shit here, and then used our best talents to cook it up in the best way possible. But in the end, we still wind up with shit. It's just cooked now, but still not very tasty."

"You're just a fountain of bad news."

"Don't blame the messenger," Angelo reminded his friend with a wicked smile. "Blame the message…"

* * *

MARK'S JOURNAL:

Until the day I die I will always remember those words coming from my friend Angelo. They will forever echo throughout my being because I will never know who to ever blame for their cruel finality.

One minute we were sitting around outside the palace and doing nothing but just passing the time and daydreaming about what we were all going to do when we got home. Then we got a call and were scrambled out on the road in a matter of minutes. A convoy of Humvees sped over to Al Hilla and into a crowded downtown area where a large chanting crowd had formed. They didn't wave to welcome us, and there definitely were no children offering flowers. There was very evident hostility in the eyes of those we passed and what they were chanting certainly wasn't friendly.

A group of Marines had surrounded a Humvee in the middle of the street and their weapons were trained on the crowd. We quickly reinforced them as the MA people moved in behind us.

A lone Marine had been driving through heavy traffic and the congestion had slowed his vehicle to a halt. An Iraqi had walked up to the Humvee, pulled out a gun and shot the Marine point blank right in the head, killing him. The crowd appeared to actually be approving of this act, which was more than a bit unnerving. We heard later from some eyewitnesses that it hadn't been an Iraqi man after all. It was a young boy who had done it, and he wasn't even in his teens.

We got the Marine's body out of there as quickly as possible and our convoy left to a barrage of taunts and thrown rocks. If any of the crowd had fired a weapon I would hate to think what would've happened to them. Captain Dylan, Angelo, and myself were in the Humvee leading the convoy back toward Babylon and we were all looking forward to getting back to the safety of our camp just as soon as possible.

The Captain and I were still discussing what a tense situation we'd left, when only a few miles away from camp bullets started flying at us from everywhere. I could hear them hit the metal of the Humvee's body and our return fire immediately burst out from Angelo and the convoy's other gunners. I sped up along the road, hoping we weren't driving into a bigger ambush ahead while the Captain called in air support.

The incoming fire started to diminish after a few moments, then an explosion suddenly lifted up the left rear of the Humvee. There was really nothing I could do to avoid what happened. It all just hit us so fast.

We rolled on our side, flipped over completely, and came to rest upright on the side of the road. Neither I nor the Captain blacked out, but we were both dazed and bleeding from cuts. Other Marines rushed over to help and pulled us out in case it exploded.

But just as it quickly became apparent that both the Captain and I were all right, it was clear from all the urgent shouts for medical help that Angelo was not.

His body was completely limp as they pulled him out of the vehicle, bleeding heavily from shrapnel wounds to the upper body, neck, and where his helmet protection ended. I screamed out his name but he couldn't respond to me then, and he never would again.

My brother in arms, Private First Class Angelo Francis Cicci of Chicago, Illinois had died instantly, less than a month before he was ticketed to go home. He'll be going home a lot sooner now, but not nearly in the way any of us expected. He was perhaps the strongest, toughest, and happiest of us all. There will never be any justice seeing his great fire extinguished on a dusty road in the middle of nowhere, somewhere south of Baghdad.

My best friend is dead, and I do not for the life of me know whom to blame. All I know is that Angelo died in a land which has always been at war, and didn't deserve a single precious American life, especially his.

September 2003

Three teary-eyed Marines squatted around the banks of the Euphrates. On one hand, it looked like a beautiful day. On the other hand, their world was as cold and dark and bleak as it ever had been.

"It's my fault, I know it is…"

"Larry, what are you talking about?"

"Mark, I come from a very religious family and I know you should never curse someone with your words because it might come true. I don't know how many times I told Angelo he was a dead man walking when he pissed me off. This is definitely on me."

"Don't be crazy, Larry!" argued Mark as the three Marines sat along the riverbank, their eyes red with tears. "We all told Angelo to eat shit and die almost on a daily basis but it didn't happen, did it? He threw it all back at us, even a lot worse."

Sykes raised his head from between his knees.

"I saw the bastards who probably killed Angelo pop up a second or two before they started firing on us. I know they're the ones who set off that bomb by remote control. If I had been able to waste them this might never have happened. It all happened so fast."

"You want someone to blame?" argued Mark. "I'm as guilty as anyone. Angelo begged me three times to change up with him. I knew he'd just keep whining about it and I'd give in sooner or later, but I thought I'd just string it out as long as I could and pay him back some of the grief he's always giving me. Maybe he had a bad feeling today, a premonition or something? If so, he obviously wouldn't have gotten any sympathy from me. I'd just figure he was playing me as usual. Maybe if he had been driving the way he always did, never in a straight line for too long, we wouldn't even have been hit in the first place?"

"You think it would be any better if Sykes and Angelo and I were down here by the river crying about you being dead?" asked Valdespino.

"Who says I'd be dead? Only God knows."

"Speaking of which," interjected Sykes, "when I was talking to the Captain he said he wanted all of us to make a point of talking to the Chaplain."

"Sounds like a really good idea," nodded Mark.

"I'll go see him then," agreed Valdespino. "But I can't be completely absolved from my sins until I get home and confess to my own priest."

"First Sergeant in the house," announced Sykes.

First Sergeant Ralston strode up to them, walking a little slower than usual. He nodded and kneeled down a few feet away from them, his eyes moving out across the river. He seemed reflective, which surprised the three Marines who had only seen him wild-eyed and possessed with high intensity before.

"I hope you men aren't sitting down here beating yourselves up about this," offered the First Sergeant in a lowered voice. "This is what I hope, but I know the truth is probably going to be something else entirely. You should know you could not possibly be beating yourself up any worse than Captain Dylan is doing to himself right now. I've known the man a good long time and I've never seen him in this state before."

"What's the Captain blaming himself for? It was my fault!" admitted Sykes with a lump in his throat.

"No, it was me!" argued Mark.

"I'm who screwed up!" piped up Valdespino.

"Men...please," soothed Ralston in a calming tone of voice they had never known to even exist in him. "Listen to me, it isn't anyone's fault, not yours, not mine, not Captain Dylan's. Every officer hopes while in war all of the men, the brothers in arms who serve under his command, will get to go back home alive. With some officers it's a bit of an ego thing to make them feel they must've done a good job preserving the lives of their Marine's, but with your Captain it's a hell of a lot more personal. He lives vicariously through you men because he used to be one of you. He just didn't lose a Marine. The Captain, he lost a brother too."

First Sergeant Ralston rose to his feet, turned and walked away without another word. The three Marines on the bank of the river felt tears starting to flow again as they looked at each other. Sykes scratched angrily, shaking his head and quickly got up to leave.

"I have to go and find this Chaplain guy."

"Tell him I'm right behind you."

"Me three," nodded Mark, his eyes in tears.

*   *   *

The phone rang and Dante set groceries on the kitchen counter and hurried into the to answer it.

"Hello?"

There was silence on the other end of the line.

"Dad," came a soft greeting in a shaky voice.

"It's Mark!" Dante shouted out to Stephanie. "Are you all right? Why haven't you called?"

"It's only been a week or so," replied Mark on a windy night from inside the communications trailer.

"It's been two and a half weeks!"

"I'm sorry."

"Never mind that. My God, at least you're alive! When Frank heard about Angelo he called to see if you were all right and we've been out of our minds not knowing anything. Of course, we haven't been able to get any information out of the military, although your mother apparently thinks her Senator is banging on the defense Secretary's door even as we speak. You don't even want to know what Emmy has been like."

"I'm so sorry. I didn't know if anyone even knew about it yet. I just haven't felt like talking."

"You're all right, you weren't injured?" asked Dante as Stephanie slipped under an arm to hug him.

"Not physically. The Captain and I were lucky. We have a few cuts and bruises, but nothing serious."

"I don't know what I can say to make you feel any better," ventured Dante. "Except maybe to let you know as long as you're alive, your family is all going to be emotionally better, even if you can't be right now. Probably isn't much consolation to you right now, but-"

"No, it is…"

"To your family it's more than consolation. I know you couldn't possibly feel the same way under the circumstances, but a lot of tears being shed in this family are quickly going to become tears of joy now."

"I appreciate it Dad, even if it doesn't sound like I do. How is Angelo's family doing?"

"Like any family in America getting the same horrible news, they're absolutely devastated."

"Captain Dylan has taken this just as hard as the rest of us. Just so you won't worry as much, we've sort of been rotated out of field operations since we're short-timers now. The Captain says it's normal to do this but we know he's just making it easier on us."

"I hope you'll start feeling better soon."

"The only thing feeling good right now is just hearing your voice again."

"Mark…"

"Don't worry, I'll be home soon. I'll call you again tomorrow. I promise."

"Don't worry? Sorry, but I can't promise that."

*   *   *

Down by the river, with the Palace of Babylon serving as the backdrop behind them, Captain Dylan crouched down to address the sitting men in his company as the overhead sunrise sky burned an orange glow as the sun started to rise over the eastern hills.

"Sure, it would've been a great thrill to blast into Baghdad with some of the forward units and cut through Iraqi defenses hand-to-hand like they were butter. Some of the Marines who actually did that are camped here at the palace and I for one love hearing their stories because they are the realities upon which Marine lore is glorified and preserved. But let me make you Devil Dogs completely aware of another reality, and that is most of the officers in those companies cannot fathom what we've been through seeing all the Marines who have died and picking up their body parts or helping un-earth mass graves. They had tanks and artillery and air support and it's what we expected to do, and if we had the same support in a similar situation would've kicked ass too, but how could my Marines do what they had to? They must be some tough ass, cold-hearted killers!'"

"Hoo-rah!" shouted the company of Marines.

"The key to our success here in Iraq," pointed out Captain Dylan, "was good training, communication, and adherence to the Corps code. As a reward for your bravery you are being sent home today."

"HOO-RAH!"

"I know many of you might be concerned about the three hundred mile drive through increasingly hostile territory to get to Kuwait City and fly home," nodded the Captain while reading the collective minds of his Marines. "So in order to ease those concerns, the Colonel and I have arranged for you all to be transported down to Kuwait City on a C-130 transport."

A prolonged cheer erupted from the company.

"I do envy you men and truly wish I could be accompanying you home," continued the Captain, "but your Lieutenant, Second Lieutenant, Staff Sergeant, and First Sergeant will safely escort you there. My replacement here has been delayed for a few weeks, but I too will be going home soon."

Protests were voiced within the company and the Captain smiled, obviously flattered. He nodded his thanks for the Marines' concern for his welfare.

"In parting, just let me say that some people think liberty is an option, but the United States of America through its armed forces believes liberty is a right worth dying for. If any of you felt differently or had not considered the costs involved in defending freedom, you would not have signed on to wage war in a country which increasingly seems to forget those who have given them the freedom to dissent against anything, including our continued presence here."

"We did not have an easy job to do here by any means, and it will be very hard to forget all the horrors we have witnessed. But what I will never forget about Iraq is the face of everyone here today, and especially the faces of those we lost. I will never forget your dedication to duty, your courage, your compassion to others, your humor, intensity, resolve, tenacity, or your satisfaction in knowing what you were doing was just and needed, and well beyond the criticism of those who haven't been here to know any better."

"As an officer and a gentleman, it is I who will salute all of you today. As long as I live, I will never be more proud of any group of men or Marines…"

*   *   *

MARK'S JOURNAL:

One day if I have children, should they ever ask me about Babylon or Iraq or this war, I will tell them I have been there, but maybe not the circumstances why.

Mesopotamia has always been known as the cradle of life, but I have also experienced it as a huge vessel of death too. Anyone who knows history realizes this has been one of the bloodiest areas on the face of our world's memory, and I for one will always remember that my best friend died here. Whether it was all worth the sacrifice is up to history to debate, but from my perspective the answer is a definite no.

What will I remember most about this country?

I will remember the sights and sounds of the long metal convoy traveling from Kuwait to Baghdad.

I will remember a small village where life and death took their toll on my innocence.

I will remember the sand fleas, the flies, the brutal heat, sandstorms, and even more fleas and flies.

I will remember a little girl and the flower she gave me whose petals are preserved in this journal.

I will remember two million dollars, which was ours not even for an instant.

I will remember the colorful robes of the men and women in the cities contrasting with the rags of the peasants in the countryside.

I will remember a thousand other sights and sounds and smells which were foreign to me.

I will remember the landfill where two thousand Iraqis were slaughtered by Saddam's regime.

I will forever remember "The Mangler's" golden crew cut as he strutted up to face me one-on-one in a fighting ring near the palace of Babylon.

I will remember all the nights when we could just look up into the stars and dream about things which had nothing to do with anything happening in Iraq.

I will remember too many little red flags stuck in the ground marking body parts and death. There were always too many of them for one person to count.

I will remember the way Captain Dylan always looked at us with such confidence and pride, and how it helped make us feel a little braver each and every day.

I will remember the amazing Angelo and his bravery on a bridge in Babylon. I will remember this and a hundred thousand other things about my friend. I will never be able to forget any of it as long as I live.

* * *

MARK'S JOURNAL:

We flew into Kuwait without any problems and then a week later they sent us home on a commercial flight through Germany. I don't really regret having come to Iraq, I just regret some of what happened while I was here. I'm hopeful in the whole scheme of things this whole experience will undoubtedly make me a bigger, better, stronger and more mature person.

We'll hit San Diego tomorrow, rest up, get debriefed, and then go through a bunch of mental and physical tests to make sure we're all safe to unleash upon American society again. I still have a year left to put into the Marines, but as long as I'm home with my family for the holidays my world will be good for now.

* * *

Feeling as happy as he'd allowed himself to be for many months, Chef Dante walked through the hotel kitchens until he found the man he was looking for.

"Dudley, do you have a minute…"

The Assistant Executive Chef looked up from the fish he was cutting and nodded.

"Chef, in advance, just let me say I'm sorry for whatever it is I did, or perhaps didn't do."

"That's not why I'm here. First of all, I want to apologize for things being a little tense around here recently. I know I haven't been talking very much and my patience has been a little shorter than usual. Mark is in San Diego now so everything should be a lot better."

"Mark's back? That's great, Chef!"

"Thank you. If you're up to the task, I'm taking some time off to spend with Mark. We're going to take a road trip out to see my father in Sacramento and then we have to go out to Chicago to attend a memorial service for Mark's friend Angelo."

"Oh my God! He got killed?"

"About a month ago. I probably should've told you but I was so worried about Mark I couldn't even think straight about anything else."

"Damn, I really liked that guy. Funny dude!"

"Yes, he was…"

"Chef, since we're kind of having this little heart-to-heart here," ventured Dudley in confidence, "I don't mean to pry or overstep any bounds I may or may not have here, but I thought you might appreciate knowing what the latest scuttlebutt is going around..."

"Which is?"

"Someone saw you coming out of a restaurant with your arm firmly around our Miss Stephanie. Some PDA was observed too. What's up with that?"

October 2003

MARK'S JOURNAL:

To say it feels good to finally be home is a huge understatement. I flew into Las Vegas after dark and it was exciting to see the lights of my city again. People have all kinds of notions about Las Vegas but to me it's a great place to live. It's really not much more of a Sin City than any other big city is.

There wasn't any band waiting for me in the terminal, no banners, no throngs of people; just my Dad and Emmy, and that is exactly the way I wanted it. There were some tears shed but smiles mostly ruled. Being back in our civilization is great.

Emmy and I stayed up talking, but not really about the war in Iraq. They've both been really good about not pressing me for any grim details until I'm comfortable enough to talk about it.

Having my own room and bed again, real clothes, and anything I want to eat; these are the things making me the happiest. I know they're simple things but those are the ones you take for granted and miss the most when you're sleeping on the ground in Iraq with sand blowing in your face and fleas always trying to make a feast out of you.

Dad wanted to stay home from work and look after me, but we convinced him to go in and then we'd plan on doing something with him when he got off at night. It's great hanging out with my sister again. She always keeps me laughing. We went to the movies, shopped until we dropped, ate not very nutritious food, and sat out by the pool doing absolutely nothing.

Dad's been taking us to the restaurants of all his buddies and we've seen just about every major new stage show on the Strip. Stephanie joins us most every night when we go out and is a lot of fun to be around. Dad just totally lights up when she's around and it's something Emmy and I never saw in him before, except when he was around us and his family. It's really good to see him this way. It's like it's supposed to be.

Does being home make me forget about Iraq or what happened to Angelo? A little, but it's never really enough. I know Emmy and Dad can sense some sadness in me and are always trying to cheer me up.

Emmy is surprised I'm still writing in my journal, but I told her it has turned out to be a good way for me to talk to myself. She'd like to read it someday, if that's alright with me, but I don't know. There was one entry after Angelo died where I was really pissed off at the whole world and I think I used every dirty word I could think of, and from being around Angelo for so long there were a lot of them. Then there was the time when I wrote about every sexual experience I'd ever had. There weren't a whole lot of them, but they were memorable and I tried not to leave out any details.

After a few days Mom and Herb blew into town and it was an entirely different scenario to deal with. All weekend she was bursting into tears every time she looked at me. I love my Mom but she can be really draining emotionally. She kept insisting I come out to West Palm Beach and spend a week with them but I told her I wanted to go visit Grandpa and then there was Angelo's memorial, but afterwards maybe I could find a few days to go visit her. It seemed to satisfy her and I'm sure she's already making plans with local debutantes.

Maybe I can come up with some more excuses when we get back from Chicago. It's not that I don't want to be around her, but Herb is trying way too hard to be my buddy and I know Mom will be trying to hook me up with some sweet thing she thinks would be perfect for me to eventually procreate with. Which means they won't be anywhere near my type. What is my type of girl? I sure hope to find out someday.

I went in to work with Dad one day and all the people there were really nice to me. He let me dress up in a chef's uniform and follow Dudley around most of the day while he did all the dirty work for Dad. It's really interesting to see what goes on in big kitchens like they have in hotels. Feeding ten or twenty thousand people a day is a lot of work and there are a ton of different things to keep your eye on. Dudley is a real trip, but I'll bet he can really drive Dad crazy.

After a week at home, Dad and I took a road trip to California. He let me drive his BMW, which was really cool. We didn't talk much, just listened to music and sports talk radio. We got to Grandpa's in the afternoon and spent a few hours with him, which was a lot of fun since he's such a crack-up. Dad left us alone to go question Grandpa's nurse about what he's been up to. Grandpa's a lot older than I remembered but his mind is still pretty sharp. He wasn't shy about asking me what went on in Iraq, if I'd been shot at or killed anyone. When my answers were vague he said he understood. Grandpa fought in Korea and experienced a lot there, so I believe he really does understand what it was like better than most. It's a comforting thought to know someone close has been through hell too.

We leave for Chicago in a few days and I have very mixed feelings about going there. I want to honor Angelo, but it's going to be kind of weird being around his family. I don't know any of them, yet I feel like I do since Angelo told me stories about everyone and

everything they did. That's what our nights were like in
Iraq. We'd lay awake in the dark telling stories about
the places and people and memories we'd left behind. I
got to come home to those people and things and he
didn't. It will always haunt me wherever I am, whatever
I do, how old I am, or who I may eventually become.

* * *

Cars lined the parking lot and surrounding
streets of the Cicci Family Funeral Home in a Chicago
suburb. Dante was dressed in a dark blue suit and Mark
wore his dress uniform as they entered a building with
a cathedral ceiling where solemn music played.

Mr. Cicci, who was even taller than his pictures
suggested, greeted Dante with a handshake and gave
Mark both a handshake and a hug before escorting them
to their seats. Mark's eyes quickly focused on the
Marine uniforms sitting in the crowd. It looked like
fully half of their company was in attendance. Oliver
Ralston was there with a wife and three young
daughters, sitting next to Captain Dylan and Caressa.
Mr. Cicci parked them one row back where Valdespino
sat holding his son Felix with wife Bettina at his side.
Sykes and his girl sat next to the Valdespinos.

Greetings were exchanged all around and Dante
seemed pleased to meet Captain Dylan, First Sergeant
Ralston, Sykes, and Valdespino. He thanked them for
all they'd done, presumably helping keep his son alive.

Mark looked around the room, identifying
people with their names and deeds from the pictures
and stories Angelo told. His Nonna smiled at Mark and
others nodded his way, but one in particular kept
looking his way. She had auburn hair and was even
prettier than any of the pictures Angelo had of his girl

Terri. Mark turned away, not knowing what he could possibly say to her as Mr. Cicci walked to the podium.

"My family is forever in the business of death and mourning, and business has not been good recently," began a somber but dignified Frank Cicci as he looked out over the room with moistened eyes. "Even though our service is built upon providing comfort to the bereaved I can't possibly give adequate comfort to my family now in their time of need because I'm in just as big of an emotional mess as they all are. This is the second and perhaps not the last memorial service in my son's honor. The first was three days after we received very horrible news. We have a multitude of tears in this family to shed for our dear Angelo and are not shy about expressing it. This is how we will all hopefully get through it…"

Angelo's father took a pause to collect himself.

"I would like to greatly express our family's appreciation to everyone here for coming from all over this great country of ours to honor my son. I would like to extend special thanks to all the brave men in our Armed Services who grace our presence today. In particular, we welcome many of the Marines who served with Angelo in Iraq, as well as their families. My wife and I, my sons and daughters, and the rest of our family and friends have had the opportunity to share memories of Angelo. But as hard as it seems, every day we remember something else that was just pure Angelo. Now, Marine Captain Jeffrey Dylan would like to come say a few words. Captain Dylan…"

Captain Dylan's hand left Caressa's as he got up and slowly walked to the front of the assembly. He was no stranger to addressing large groups and quickly took command of the room as his eyes sought out different eyes in the crowd with every word he spoke.

"Bold, audacious, witty, brave, determined, committed, profane, vain, compassionate, selfish, caring, fearless, concerned, talkative, arrogant, sweet, loving, smart, loyal, opinionated, exasperating, proud, helpful, playful, challenging, hopeful, friendly, contemptible, funny, trusting, distrusting, humble, wise, brash, and unforgettable. By themselves these are just words, but together they made up a very complicated but utterly delightful young man I was proud to have served under my command in the United States Marines. Angelo Cicci could be the instigator of various stunts and pranks, the life of the party, a real pain in the ass sometimes, but also someone you could trust your life with. He was completely unafraid, questioned everything, followed orders to the best of his ability, pushed the envelope as far as he could in all situations, and claimed to be eminently knowledgeable on almost any subject anyone dared to bring up in his presence. He was, in the terminology all Marines share, always good to go…"

"My company of Marines experienced all the horrors of war from Nasiriyah and Diwaniyah to Baghdad, Hilla, Karbala, and Babylon. We were fortunate to have only lost one of our brothers in the eight months we were deployed in Kuwait and Iraq. Unfortunately, the Marine we lost was Angelo Francis Cicci, and in a way he was among the best of us."

"His instincts were always good, his heart was in the right place, and he did things none of the rest of us would ever contemplate doing," explained Captain Dylan. "Angelo was all about action and one incident in particular illustrates what the Angelo we knew and loved was really all about. It was one of the bravest things a person could do, but perhaps one of the least sensible too when you put your life on the line for something which transcends war. But Angelo didn't see things the way anyone else did. He followed his heart and instincts and sensibility to the point where the thought of losing his life for someone he didn't even know, never even crossed his mind. What he did is yet another validation of why we had to go to Iraq and help those people. I wasn't there with Angelo the day of this particular incident, but his best friend Private Mark Sebastian was. Mark, would you come up and share a few words about your friend and that experience?"

Mark hesitated, but after a nod from his father got up and reluctantly made his way up to the front of the room. Captain Dylan gave him a supportive handshake as they passed. Mark got up to the podium and initially had a hard time raising his eyes. Finally, he summoned the courage to look up and face them all.

"This is probably the hardest thing I've ever had to do in my life, and even though Angelo is gone now, I'm still going to blame this on him anyway."

Soft laughter eased the mood in the room.

"On the way over here I was telling my Dad the reason why this was going to be so hard is not just because it's about Angelo, but because it's about all of you, his family and friends. You may not know me, but I feel like I know most of you rather well. Angelo made sure of that. You were all very special to him, so he made you special to all of us too. I too come from a strong, supportive family. We just don't have the massive numbers you do. But Angelo invited us to be part of his extended family, and we were glad to be included in Angelo's family stories because we would all sit there smiling and attentive while he told about Uncle Tony's latest misadventure, or how Angelo used to glue his brother's toes together while he was sleeping when they were younger, then blow smoke into the fire alarm to wake him up so he'd fall on his butt."

More laughter spread and Mark singled out a twelve-year-old boy in the crowd. "While in Iraq we faithfully followed Rocco Junior's little league season as he batted four-twenty-nine with six homers and thirty one runs batted in, enroute to the championship."

Young Rocco nodded back proudly. Mark's eyes caught Terri's momentarily before moving on to Nonna.

"Okay," asked Mark, warming up to the task, "so how many of you know the secret ingredient Nonna Cicci puts in her famous veal and eggplant dish? What's it called again, Dad?"

"Vitello Melanzane," called out his father.

"How many of you know the secret ingredient?"

Only a few hands were raised in the crowd. Mark slowly raised his hand, closing his eyes while nodding his head. Nonna Cicci gasped, horrified that her secret had been shared outside the family.

"Don't worry," Mark assured her, "Angelo swore me to secrecy. But if I ever learn how to cook…"

More laughter was shared. Nonna Cicci smiled up to Mark and waved her rosary beads in blessing.

"The point I'm trying to make here is that whether your name is Frank or Bruno or Angela or Gina or Rocco or Luigi or Tony or Sophia or Little Mike or Giacomo or Terri, all of the Marines in this room know a lot more about you than you probably think, and I like to think we're all a little better for it."

Mark paused, remembering the incident.

"Please understand, we had a few really bad days in Iraq, for sure. But most of our days were pretty good considering the circumstances. Some days were even downright boring, and when we needed a change Angelo was usually the first to let us know it. I remember it was a hot sunny day just like most others in Iraq, and we'd all been sitting around arguing about whether eastern or southern or northern or western or southwestern barbeque sauce was better. Angelo claimed his big brother Gino's barbecue sauce was hands down the best and wanted to prove it to us."

Gino clasped both hands up in victory.

"The problem was there wasn't any chicken we could get our hands on at the camp, and pork didn't really exist in Iraq. So Angelo somehow got permission from the Captain to go into the town of Babylon, pick up some of the local variety, and see if we could scare up the makings for some barbeque sauces. The only reason the Captain gave us the okay was because things were relatively calm and he wanted to put Gino's sauce to the test against his family's own Carolina-style vinegar recipe. So the four of us jumped into a Humvee, and by the four of us I mean Angelo, Hilario Valdespino the Marine right there holding his new son Felix and wife, Corporal Jimmy Sykes who's sitting right next to him with his wife, and me."

All eyes turned to identify the Marines.

"Now, we're all carrying M-16 rifles and have a 50 caliber *Ma Deuce* machine gun on top of our vehicle so this is definitely not how most people go to the market, at least not here," continued Mark. "But Captain Dylan always reinforced the message about us being careful at all times, wherever we were. So we parked in downtown Babylon near this bridge and Hilario and Jimmy stayed with our vehicle while Angelo and I went hunting for a market of some kind. We finally found one about a block and a half away and after some serious haggling by Angelo, who had picked up enough of the local lingo to intelligently argue about prices, we finally walked out of the store with six freshly killed and plucked Babylonian chickens."

Mark's mood then turned serious.

"When we got about half a block away from the Humvee we started to hear a lot of gunfire coming from exactly the direction where we were going. So Angelo and I ran up with fingers on our triggers because we didn't know what was going on. We had to ditch the chickens along the way since it was starting to sound like a major firefight ahead."

"Valdespino and Sykes were crouched behind the Humvee taking fire across the bridge while another squad of Marines on the other side of the street as us fired back at a bunch of Iraqis on the other side of the bridge who had AK-47 rifles and a machine gun. Angelo and I ran to cover behind the Humvee and everyone started firing. It was totally unexpected and dangerously crazy."

"Later, we came to find out the other Marines had detained some suspects and were questioning them when a group of insurgents opened fire on them. When they saw our Humvee they opened up on it too."

"So we're all trading fire diagonally across this bridge and anyone who is on it is in real danger. Cars were stopped and passengers crouched down inside, and people walking on the bridge hit the ground. Everyone that is, except for this one little old lady shuffling her way right into the line of fire. She was covered in black from head to foot. Maybe she couldn't hear or see too well. I guess we'll never really know."

"But Angelo saw her and reacted instinctively, as we are trained to do. He immediately started to move up toward the bridge and told us to cover him. I told him he was crazy but he wouldn't listen. He took off on a mad dash toward the bridge and now the rest of us really had to do something. I'm firing away, Hilario is launching grenades across the bridge, and Sykes is up in the Humvee letting loose with the machine gun."

"I thought for sure Angelo was going to get killed, and in turn so might the rest of us. But somehow Angelo cheated fate and a lot of bullets, and made it safely up to the old woman. He pulled the old lady gently down to the ground, dragged her over behind a car, and then for some unfathomable reason he got back up and charged to the bridge railing while firing away at the Iraqis like some fearless angry warrior madman straight out of a movie! Killed a bunch of them!"

Mark nodded to the *oohs* and *aahs* coming from the room as the picture hit them all.

"We killed more of them and the rest ran off, so after a few very long minutes everything was back to normal. Angelo went back and helped the old lady up and she brushed his arm away, then shuffled off without even thanking him. Then to make matters worse, the chickens were gone when we went back to get them and we were out of money. I was madder at Angelo than I'd ever been, which is saying a lot, and demanded to know what prompted him to do what he did. Why risk your life on someone you don't even know, who doesn't even mean much in the whole scheme of things?"

Mark tried to imitate Angelo's voice.

"He said '*Shark, she was someone, she was someone's Grandma*'. Then he proceeded to tell me the story about how his own dear Nonna was walking home from a market in the old neighborhood a long time ago and got caught in the crossfire between two rival street gangs. One of the gang members stopped firing and risked his life to pull her out of harm's way. Angelo, in his own way, was simply paying back a good deed."

A completely surprised Nonna Cicci started to bawl inconsolably. Angelo's father and mother were both tearful, but pride was shining brightly in Frank Cicci's eyes as he shook his head at relatives and then nodded that it sounded like something his son would do. Mark looked out and was hard pressed to find a dry eye in the room. He smiled through his own tears.

"Angelo did get his butt chewed out pretty good when we got back to camp, not for what he did but for perhaps risking his life rather needlessly. Since we totally missed the mess call we all had to eat MREs for lunch. But knowing the way Angelo operated, I have no doubt if the same situation ever happened again, he'd probably handle it the same way. I for one, choose to respect this, the true intent of his heart. Thank you."

Mark had nothing else left to say and hurried off the podium. He could see tears in people's eyes but the only ones that stuck with him were the ones streaming down from Angelo's girlfriend Terri. He sat down next to his father while the other Marines, including Captain Dylan, whispered praises toward him.

Frank Cicci returned to the podium, somehow smiling through his tears.

"Thank you, Mark, that was really something special. You've been a very good friend to my son. He considered you his brother. What you have shared with us about him will always be part of Cicci family lore."

*   *   *

After the service ended everyone retreated a few blocks away to the expansive backyard of the Cicci estate where a lavish buffet was presented to the guests.

Dante went off to talk with Captain Dylan, Caressa, First Sergeant Ralston, and both Valdespino's and Sykes families. Mark felt the need to be alone as he looked over grounds where his good friend had lived.

"Quite nice, isn't it?"

"Yes Sir. Makes me wonder why Angelo would ever want to leave all of this to go fight in Iraq?"

"Believe me, his family had the same opinion. Our family worked hard to get where we are, so our children would have better options in life. But our Angelo walked to the beat of a different drummer. He had his own agenda. He was very special..."

"Yes Sir."

"Mark, my wife and I truly appreciate the words you said. When all you really have left are memories they become even more precious. You do know a lot about all of us, but we also know a lot about you. All Angelo ever did when he called or wrote or e-mailed us was tell stories about his fellow Marines and their families. But I may have erred when I shared one of those particular stories with your father."

"What story was that?" asked Mark, worried. "Not the one about those girls in Las Vegas, I hope."

"You and Angelo scored some babes in Vegas?" Frank Cicci smiled, impressed. "No, I hadn't heard about that one, but I might like to. The story I heard was about an ambush in Iraq where you saved Angelo and a lot of other Marines' lives and single-handedly killed twenty Iraqi soldiers. Your father didn't seem to know anything about it."

"Sir, you know Angelo was prone to exaggerate. There were only thirteen and not all were..."

"Oh, there were *only thirteen* of them?" said an astonished Mr. Cicci. "Well, if it was *only thirteen* then I guess it all becomes irrelevant. Thank you anyway for saving my son's life."

"It wasn't like that, Sir..."

"Chef Dante, I need your professional opinion," called out Frank Cicci to Mark's father. "There is a raging debate in our family over which is better, our Nonna's almost secret Vitello Melanzane or my brother Tony's Linguine Tutto Mare? Let us go inside and put this question to rest once and for all."

"Freaking Angelo!" muttered Mark.

"Hello…"

Mark spun around at the sound of her voice and there she was, looking as lovely as any young woman could possibly be.

"I'm Teresa, or Terri if you like…" she smiled.

"I like, I mean…I know who you are."

"You do?"

"Sure, from Angelo's stories, his pictures, even from his dreams…"

"I hope he didn't exaggerate too many of them."

"I think we both knew him better than that. Don't worry, he never ever said anything bad about you, but whether or not he ever bent the truth, you'll have to tell me. I always thought of Angelo as this playboy wannabe, so when he told me he was planning to come home and get married after you graduated high school, it really kind of floored me."

"What?" Terri seemed completely surprised.

"He was planning to marry you when he came home. He never mentioned it?"

"No, of course not!" she said, almost in shock. "We wrote back and forth and flirted a little in our letters, but that was just Angelo and I wanted to make him feel loved and less lonely. What's this about graduating? I graduated in June of last year."

"So you're not…like sixteen or seventeen?"

"Do I look that age?" she asked, just a little offended. "I'm eighteen going on nineteen. I swear,

Angelo could drive a person crazy! He would get things into his head and they'd stick in there whether they were true or not!"

"I know exactly what you mean," laughed Mark. "So, you would have turned him down?"

"Of course I would!" Terri shook her head and tried to explain. "Mark, Angelo was like my brother and I will always love him. I did have a crush on him when I was fourteen or fifteen, but Angelo was a bad boy where girls were concerned, and he's definitely not the kind of man I would ever want to marry. He was like a lot of the guys around here. They say they love you, marry you, and then soon start cheating on you. They go to church, confess, repent their sins, then go out and repeat the same cycle all over again. Thank you, but no thanks."

"I didn't expect to hear anything like this from you," Mark was in a relative state of shock. "Angelo seemed like he was really in love with you. I thought you'd be heartbroken when I finally met you."

"I am heartbroken Mark, but not for the reason you thought. Is that why you looked away from me every time our eyes met?"

"Basically, yes. I came to Chicago not wanting to talk to you more than anyone else," he admitted. "I didn't know what I could say to make you feel better since you'd lost what I thought was your intended."

"I didn't know if I'd have the courage to come up and talk to you either," she confessed. "I mean, you're 'The Shark' and Angelo told everyone about how cool and brave you are. He really looked up to you, which is a truly rare and very surprising thing for someone like Angelo."

"Brave? I was scared shitless most of the time I was over there. Guess I hid it well."

"You did look a little scared when you had to go up and talk about Angelo, but you made it through with flying colors, which I thought was a pretty brave, cool thing to do. This tall, good-looking Marine walks in with his handsome father, and I saw right away how well the other Marines regarded you," reflected Terri, admiration glowing in her green eyes. "It was a really tough room to play. The Cicci family is not an easy crowd to win over. Believe me, I know. But first you had them all laughing, and then you made everyone cry. I was wiping away tears and immediately telling myself I just had to meet you."

"I still feel real sorry for Angelo," said Mark, beginning to have the strangest feeling as their eyes were seemingly locked together.

"Why? He would've got over any rejection very easily," she assured him. "Look around Mark, there are at least a dozen girls here I know Angelo slept with. I wasn't ever going to join the list. By the way, I just want to warn you they'll all be throwing themselves at you just as soon as they guzzle enough wine to lose whatever inhibitions they might still have."

"I'm not looking for any of that," he confided to her, uneasy with the prospect. "To tell you the truth, I don't really know what I'm looking for. But I do have to tell you the reason I really still feel sorry for Angelo is because you are absolutely gorgeous, and sweeter than any picture or memory could ever do justice to."

Terri was obviously flattered by his words, if not charmed. She momentarily lost her breath and smile before quickly regaining both with an added pulse.

"Thank you, Mark. I don't think anyone has ever said anything nicer to me. Is it really true what you said about not knowing what you're looking for?"

"I'm desperately in search of direction now."

Terri held his eyes for a moment, then smiled.

"Well, I sure like the way you're looking at me right now. Why don't you just start there?"

Mark felt himself smiling for the first time in a very long while.

"How would you like to go inside and toast a few drinks to our friend?" asked Mark, both relieved and excited. "Maybe you can help protect me from Angelo's pack of she-devils…"

"I'd love to…"

He offered her his arm and she quickly took it to be escorted inside.

* * *

MARK'S JOURNAL:

Am I really wrong to be feeling the way I do now? I went to Chicago dreading the thought and came back feeling something I've never felt before. Angelo had told me so many good things about Terri and the type of person she was that I was envious of him finding someone like her. I used to think *Where's my Terri and when will I find her?* Well, I found her and it was the exact same person I'd come to know through Angelo. Only she wasn't really Angelo's girl after all.

We stayed together all evening. Eating, drinking, talking, laughing, and crying. The Cicci's really know how to throw a party. Terri is gorgeous and sweet and sassy and everyone from my Dad to Captain Dylan and Caressa and Jimmy and the Valdespinos told me how great she was. Dad was looking at me like *what is going on with you, Mark? You can't take your eyes off this girl.* I couldn't, it was impossible for me to. I think her parents liked me too. When the party broke up and she had to go home I really wanted to kiss her good night but was afraid to try. She gave me a big hug and I definitely want to be in that position again, with my arms around her and her arms around me. I'm hopeful the kisses will come.

The next day Dad and I were going to play tourists in Chicago and Terri volunteered to be our guide. The sights and sounds of Chicago are cool but all I seem to remember about the day is how she looked and the sound of her voice. After dinner Dad quickly got the hint and retired to his room to call Stephanie. Terri and I went out for a walk. The night was cool but clear and we sat by the lake talking like old friends with the lights of Chicago behind us. Neither of us knew what was happening between us, only it was very apparent that something definitely was. It was a real surprise to us both, but somehow it just felt right and we both wanted to see where it would lead.

When I finally kissed her good night it seemed like the most natural thing in the world to do. When we kissed some more I knew I'd found something I'd want to do every time I saw her again. I've kissed girls before but no one has ever kissed me the way she did, and no one will until I'm with her again.

We promised to write, e-mail, and phone as much as we can. I may not see her for a month or so, which is going to be tough. I spent eight months in a hellhole called Iraq and now four weeks seems like an eternity to me before I can see her again.

I took a chance and asked her to be my date at the Marine Corps Ball in San Diego in early December. She immediately said yes, which I will interpret as being a good sign. I also asked her to come to Las Vegas over New Years and she's already bought her ticket to fly in the day after Christmas. I really want Emmy to meet her.

Teresa Marie Anthony is absolutely amazing and even though I just met her, I've never felt this way about anyone before in my life. Life is really a trip and I'm glad to be on it again. Just when things are starting to look up, something bad can happen unexpectedly. Then when you think you're down and out, in an instant someone can walk into your life and lift your heart up higher than you ever thought it could fly.

November 2003

MARK'S JOURNAL:

For a while I didn't even want to read the newspapers about what was still happening in Iraq. I wanted to make it out of sight, out of mind. But lately I've been taking more of an interest. Dad thinks the President won't be re-elected, that he'll be a one-term wonder just like his father was. I'm not so sure, but things aren't looking too good for him right now.

I read where the lack of support in the Pentagon is threatening the administration's plans in Iraq. They admit there is no evidence linking Saddam to 9/11, but say there's no question he had ties to Al Qaeda.

The President's approval rating is the lowest it's been since right before 9/11. Only 50% of those polled approve of the job he's doing in Iraq. If they took the same poll in Iraq using the soldiers and Marines who are still over there, I'm sure the numbers would even be lower. More soldiers die every day from insurgent attacks and neither the administration nor the Pentagon seems to have a good handle on how to stop it.

Apparently the economy is starting to grow again, but the President is warning us after a recession employment is usually the last thing to rise, which somehow doesn't make any sense to me. I know we are buying lots of ammunition, MREs, Humvees, bombs, and cruise guided missiles so at least the defense sector of the job market is apparently doing all right.

The media is saying the White House may have to go back to the United Nations and ask for help in Iraq. It might be a tough sell considering we invaded without their approval, and why should it be their responsibility to help us when it wasn't their idea to go in there in the first place? If we had at least found some weapons of mass destruction then maybe we could justify it all, and other countries might feel we were right to attack Iraq. It's not looking that way right now. I remember last year when the President said the UN was flirting with irrelevance when they wouldn't back his move into Iraq. He might be eating those words soon. I'm just glad I'm safely home and not still in the middle of the meat grinder.

Terri and I have got to the point where we talk at least once every day, but usually more. I just like hearing her voice, but I also ask her opinion on stuff because she's pretty smart and level headed. She's taking a semester off to work but wants to go into hospitality management so she can maybe run a hotel someday, like Stephanie does. I told her I was seriously considering going to culinary school and she thinks it's a great idea. Obviously there is potential for our career paths to cross some day. We both like the idea of that.

She's flying out to Las Vegas on Friday the sixth of December and Dad is letting me borrow the BMW to drive down to San Diego on Saturday morning. The Ball is Saturday night so we'll stay somewhere that night and then drive back on Sunday. When I told Terri we were going to get a hotel room she was quiet but didn't seem to have a real problem with it. The only alternative would be to drive back to Las Vegas after midnight and neither one of us wants to do that. I'm getting a little nervous about it already. It's not like anything has to happen if we spend the night together, but if I start kissing her it's going to be hard to stop.

* * *

Dante headed out the front door and saw Mark very relaxed, stretched out watching tv.

"Mark, I'm going out for lunch with Stephanie. Is there anything I can pick up for you?"

"No thanks, I'm very fine," said his contented son. "Just going to sit here and watch the tube. There's this show I want to watch called *Three Voices*. I hear they really get into some good arguments about Iraq."

"I've seen it before. It's been a pretty bad month over in Iraq. When you were over there I watched the news religiously, but now that you're home I really don't pay much attention to it any more."

"I've kind of been that way too, Dad, but we're starting to take heavy casualties so it's hard for me to just ignore it completely. We're going to have to go on the offensive again and really pound them hard or they'll keep picking us off for as long as we're there."

"I wish we had a solution to the problem. All I know is, it's great to have you home."

"I agree completely."

"Terri called while you were at the gym."

"She told me. I called her a little while ago."

"Is everything going well for you two?"

"Just wish I could see her sooner than later."

"I'm happy you met. She's a very nice young lady. See you later."

"Okay. Say hello to Stephanie for me."

"Will do. By the way, there's a cold game hen in the refrigerator if you get hungry. It was roasted with lemon juice and a balsamic glaze and was stuffed with risotto Milanese."

"Say no more, the Shark is on the hunt."

The front door closed and Mark surfed around for the channel he was looking for.

"Welcome to *Three Voices,*" spoke Diana Scott. "A top secret CIA report has detailed a bleak picture for America in Iraq and concludes our inability to end the resistance there will only fuel more insurgency. A growing number of Iraqis have concluded the U.S. led coalition can be defeated and are now actively supporting the resistance. The report paints a bleak picture of the political and security situation and cautions our efforts to rebuild the country into a democracy could collapse unless corrective action is immediately taken. This analysis sharply contrasts the upbeat assessment the Administration is presenting to the public as part of an increasingly aggressive publicity campaign to counter mounting criticism at home about mounting American casualties in Iraq."

Three men were at the table with her.

"Gentlemen, will plans to install a sovereign government in Iraq defuse the rebellion?"

"Not entirely, Diana. Recently there have been a lot of bad elements added to the mix," asserted General Pynchon. "Peripheral players such as foreign fighters coming in from the Syrian border, radical Shiites sneaking in from Iran, Al Qaeda, Taliban, you name it. While the dialogue must continue of course, I think some very forceful military action on our part is warranted. You can't even begin to think about having a free election until all this violence stops."

"How would you quell this?"

"You want me to put down this rebellion once and for all? I'd send Marine and Army commando units back in and give them the teeth to bite back hard. There are so many weapons in Iraq we're going to have to systematically disarm the entire country, city-by-city, town-by-town, and house-by-house. We may not find every weapon, but we'll find most of them and more importantly the people who are planning to use them against us. Sure, this is going to ruffle some feathers and a few innocent people might get hurt, but that's just too damn bad. We gave these people the opportunity to back off and do the right thing, but they've decided to resort to this hit and run terrorism. So we hit them hard, search and destroy, and see how brave they are then. Some people only understand compliance by force."

"Americans tried the same thing in Vietnam and it didn't work out too well," suggested Al Khayyam.

"Congressman Ballantree, is he right? Is Iraq about to become another Vietnam nightmare?"

"I hope not and I'm sure this isn't a correlation the White House would want anyone to make, but as the casualties continue to rise, so will the comparisons. Unfortunately, the total number of dead American servicemen in Iraq now exceeds the total for the early years of the Vietnam War."

"That's misleading Wayne, and you know it," countered the General. "Between 1962 and 1964 we had about four hundred casualties in Vietnam, about the same as we now have in Iraq. But we only had about 17,000 troops over there then, compared to the 130,000 we currently have in Iraq. So you need to put it all into the proper perspective. When we had 130,000 troops over in Vietnam in 1965 we lost over 2,000 men. Hell, in 1968 we lost 16,000 men. So in comparison to Vietnam we've suffered very few casualties in Iraq."

"There were over 50,000 total deaths in Vietnam, Fitz. So does this make it an acceptable loss for you?" Congressman Ballantree wanted to know. "The escalation of violence is what inevitably leads us into the quagmire, and I don't think your plan to go back in with both guns blazing is the answer to the problem. This is clearly an unacceptable situation for America, Iraq, and the rest of the world."

"Another concern is the thousands of men and women who are being seriously wounded which we really aren't hearing much about," offered Diana Scott.

"Good point" agreed the Congressman. "We can't just patch people up and send them back to work. They've lost limbs and mobility and have to recover from both physical injuries and any psychological damage for the rest of their lives. It's a disgrace to ignore their sacrifice because their numbers are embarrassing to the White House. The numbers of dead and wounded in action are unacceptable, and whoever is responsible needs to be held accountable. The only reason Americans still support operations in Iraq is because they know our troops didn't have any choice but to be over there."

"Saddam Hussein is the one who's responsible," explained the General. "We haven't caught him yet, but we will. Now, I'm not saying we haven't made some mistakes and this suggests there was a serious security lapse on the ground. I for one wouldn't stand for it!"

"If we can now get back to the question of Iraqi sovereignty and the electoral process," suggested Al Khayyam, "perhaps I can bring some light into the darkness. Americans envision a caucus vote, which will in fact exclude most Iraqis. The most powerful man in Iraq lives in the holy city of Najaf and he represents the 60% Shiite majority of Iraqi citizens. If he wants direct elections by next June there will be big trouble if this is not the case for any reason. True democracy rewards the majority and he definitely represents the majority."

"I'm hearing there are serious doubts it can all be organized by January of next year, much less this June," interjected the Congressman. "I'm sure everyone on the Iraqi Governing Council is taking the Grand Ayatollah's concerns seriously, but whether they can actually adopt this proposal in the right time frame is something else. I do agree the Iraqi people must have the basic role in any issues concerning the destiny of their country. It is one of the tenets of true democracy. This Administration is going to have to accept the fact we cannot expect Iraq to accept proposals putting our interests ahead of theirs."

"How in the hell do you expect to have a direct election when you don't have voter rolls?" complained the General. "You can't even create voter rolls until you conduct a census, and this takes time. We are not going to allow the election process in Iraq to be hijacked by extremist Muslim groups. We're not going to allow a Taliban-type takeover or let clerics run the country like they do in Iran. To create a democracy takes time."

"So the democracy chosen for them will not necessarily reflect the will of the people?"

"That isn't what I said, Al Khayyam! I'm simply pointing out the difference between what some people may want to do and what can actually be done. This is the reality but I'm confident there is still time to reconcile any differences through the process of open dialogue, which is now available to the Iraqi people for the first time thanks to coalition liberation efforts."

"The Shiites were the persecuted majority under the rule of Saddam Hussein," explained Al Khayyam. "Will the Shiites become the persecuted majority again in this so-called democracy just because the White House and the Kurds and the Sunni don't trust their intentions? If you return to rule by a few in Iraq then your war will have achieved nothing. Why should the majority not have most things their way? Here in America when the Republicans or Democrats control

Congress or the White House is their basic agenda not followed? If the United States did not have the common sense to understand the true determination of Iraq's future would be up to the people of Iraq and not the White House, then they should not have stuck their nose into the affairs of Iraq in the first place. There are no weapons of mass destruction in Iraq and anyone who believes Saddam Hussein was ever a direct threat to the United States has simply joined an audience of fools."

"Obviously, there have been serious mistakes made," agreed Ballantree, "and the direction we're presently heading in needs to dramatically improve. The President is going to have to do something soon because if he doesn't, he won't have an exit strategy to explain to voters in an election year. The electorate is split right down the middle now and if voters don't believe they can trust what he's saying or the direction he's taking this country, then he will be gone."

"We have time for a final comment from each of you on where the situation is heading," stated Diana Scott. "Mr. Al Khayyam?"

"Under current leadership I see a downward spiral. America sees itself as liberators with lofty democratic ideals, but much of the world, especially the Muslim world, sees America as being led by radical extremists operating from a bully pulpit. I wait to hear the next spin on Iraq, the next convenient reason to justify this invasion. First it was weapons of mass destruction, then it changed to removing a despot who was getting ready to attack your country. Now the rhetoric has changed again to some noble appearing vision of extending democracy throughout the Middle East and presumably around the world. As a Muslim, I must conclude if someone does not understand or respect our cultures then we must respectfully reject this veiled gift of democracy. The Muslim world wants no part of political maneuvering and economic conquest disguised as a moral crusade."

'Thank you very much. Congressman?"

"Under the current leadership I also see a downward spiral. Everyone is embarrassed about the way this Administration is handling the post-war climate. Both the Secretary of Defense and the Vice President are a couple of old war horses who should be put out to pasture before they do any more damage."

"Thank you, Congressman. General Pynchon?"

"The bottom line in Iraq is going to be exactly what our leaders have told us it was going to be all along. Our men and women are fighting terrorist enemies thousands of miles away in the heart and soul of their power base so we don't have to face those enemies in the heart of America. The enemy in Iraq believes America will pack up and run when the going gets tough, and this is why they're willing to keep on killing innocent civilians, relief workers, and coalition forces. But America is not going to run away from its vital mission in Iraq. We will not be deterred."

"Thank you for joining us on 'Three Voices'."

Mark tore the cold game hen in half and switched the channel over to the Food Network where Chef Emeril Lagasse was getting ready to finish a dish by throwing some red powder at it.

"*BAM*...and it's done!"

* * *

"Sure smells great in here," yawned Mark as he walked into the kitchen on a slightly chilly Thanksgiving morning in Las Vegas.

"That's always a good sign on Thanksgiving morning," said Dante as his son gave him a hug from behind. "Were you up late last night?"

"Video game madness has seemingly begun to run amok. What's on the menu today?"

"We have a Willie Bird turkey from Sonoma. They're broad-breasted, mostly white meat, and naturally grown. The stuffing is cornbread, pecans, fuji apples, herbes de provence, and three types of sausage: Italian, andouille, and chicken apple. Instead of mashed potatoes we're having Potatoes Delmonico, garlic mashers baked with Asiago cheese and breadcrumbs. Various salads, haricot verts sautéed in shallots and extra virgin olive oil, pumpkin cheesecake, and Stephanie brought her famous sweet potato casserole."

"Sounds very edible to me! Where is Steph?"

"She is out setting the table in the dining room."

"Steph!" called out Mark as he stumbled out to see her in the dining room. "Hey, you really look great! So who all is coming today?"

"You, me, your Dad, your Grandpa, his nurse Flo, and Emmy," said Stephanie after sharing a hug.

"Hmm? Looks like you set one place too many."

"Emmy is bringing home this girl who couldn't be with her family. You know how she is."

"Cool. What time will everyone be here?"

"In about an hour..."

"Guess I better take a shower and get dressed."

"Might be a good idea," she winked at him.

* * *

An hour later Mark returned to the kitchen clean-shaven, wearing slacks and a golf shirt.

"Dad, I just heard this on my radio. Guess who turned up in Baghdad for Thanksgiving dinner?"

"Saddam?"

"No, the President."

"Really?" asked Stephanie. "Sounds like it must be the official start of an election year."

"Exactly," agreed Mark. "They flew Air Force One into Baghdad International Airport at night with the lights off so no one would try and fire a missile at them. The President helped feed the troops, posed for pictures, made a speech, and then left a couple of hours later before the bad guys even knew he was there. Pretty cool for those soldiers, I guess. Or maybe not..."

Mark heard the front door open and went to see who it was. Emmy came in with Flo pushing Grandpa Marcus's wheelchair and the family patriarch smiled when his eyes found Mark.

"Buddy boy!"

"Grandpa! Hey Flo, welcome to our home."

"Thank you," she smiled. "Thought I should come and try to keep him in line."

"I've been waiting for a little discipline from you for a long time," the old man joked as Mark hugged him. "You can restrain me whenever you like."

Dante and Stephanie came out to greet them as Emmy entered and gave Mark a big hug.

"Happy Thanksgiving, Mark."

"Happy Thanksgiving, Emmy. I thought you were bringing a friend?"

"She's getting her things. Can you help her?"

"Sure..."

Mark walked out the front door and was totally shocked by who he saw standing there.

"You live here? Emmy is your sister?"

Wearing a business suit and pulling her luggage, a smiling and beautiful Terri stepped forward to kiss him and exchange an extended hug as Mark's family and friends applauded.

"Happy Thanksgiving," she whispered. "Not all dreams come true, but some really do…"

"You're telling me! I don't believe this!"

"I talked to Teresa on the phone a couple of weeks ago," explained Dante as an entirely stunned Mark led Terri into the house, "and she told me she planned to go into hospitality management so I told her about UNLV having one of the best programs in the country. So then I talked her parents into letting Teresa come out and explore her options here."

"You told me you were going out of town to have Thanksgiving with family friends?"

"So here I am. Your family are friends of my family," nodded Terri innocently.

Mark looked over at a beaming Stephanie.

"You told me Emmy was bringing home a girl who couldn't be with her family."

"She couldn't be with them when she was going to be here, could she?"

"Okay, now I get it, you're all in this together, aren't you?" Mark smiled, very appreciative of the fact. "Why, you're just a scheming bunch of rascally rabbits, aren't you?"

"I didn't have anything to do with nothing," claimed Grandpa Marcus innocently.

"We wanted you to know how thankful we are to have you home," explained Emmy, "so we decided to make it the best possible Thanksgiving for you."

"Mission accomplished!"

"Now, we will have to give Teresa back to her family after your trip to San Diego," Dad warned him.

"If it's alright with you?"

"You're staying here for *ten days*?" Mark was wide-eyed on the verge of being speechless. "This is getting better and better!"

Everyone laughed at the look on Mark's face.

"Mark," noted Emmy, "I just want to warn you Terri and I are going shopping tomorrow."

"Can't I go with you too?" pleaded Mark.

"Oh alright," agreed Emmy, feigning reluctance.

"Mark, why don't you get Teresa settled into the guest bedroom and then you can both join us in the dining room. Come on, everyone," announced Dante, "it's about time to eat."

Mark started to lead Terri away when an authoritative voice stopped him in his tracks.

"Just a minute there, buddy boy!"

"What is it, Grandpa?"

"I got to know this young lady very well on the ride over, and would like to ask you a simple question."

Grandpa Marcus began with a sly wink in Stephanie's direction. Dante shook his head, knowing exactly what to expect next.

"Okay, shoot," smiled Mark.

Grandpa Marcus cocked his head to one side and looked Mark right in the eye.

"Well, do you love her, or what?"

December 2003

"Good morning Mr. Sebastian," smiled Teresa as she walked out onto the patio hand-in-hand with Mark. Dante looked up the morning newspaper.

"Continental breakfast today," Dante motioned to the nearby covered tray. "Please help yourselves."

They both loaded up on fresh fruit, muffins, croissants, yogurt, and coffee; and brought it back to the table where they grabbed sections of the newspaper for themselves. Both were dressed casually in shorts and t-shirts. Mark snagged the entertainment section while Terri picked up the sports page. They shared breakfast, alternating bites of the food between them.

"Teresa, the sports section?" questioned Dante.

"It's football season. Are you kidding me?"

"Isn't she great, Dad?" beamed Mark.

"The way to a man's heart is sometimes right down the middle of the field. What do you two have planned for today?"

"We have to go and pick up my ball gown later."

"Dad, Emmy found this killer dress at Fashion Show Mall. It is just amazing. Okay, vision this: auburn hair, green eyes, a great body, and this completely backless purple dress."

"I think it might just work," she smiled.

"Tonight we're going to the National Finals Rodeo. Do you want to go with us?"

"Sorry, we're booked solid. Late night feeding. I'd like to read you something very strange, so prepare yourselves," said Dante as he turned the newspaper to find the right page. "Now this is a direct quote."

"Okay, go ahead…"

"Reports that say that something hasn't happened are always interesting to me, because as we know, there are known knowns, there are things we know we know. We also know there are known unknowns; that is to say we know there are some things we do not know. But there are also unknown unknowns, the ones we don't know we don't know."

"What?" wondered Mark, looking confused.

"That doesn't make any sense," agreed Terri.

"Agreed, now who said it?"

"Somebody on Saturday Night Live?"

"No, the Secretary of Defense."

"You've got to be kidding me?"

"I truly wish I was, Terri," sighed Dante, "but he uttered those same exact words at a recent press briefing in Iraq. This very comment has already won the United Kingdom's Plain English Campaign *Foot in Mouth* award for the most baffling statement by a public figure. Maybe ever."

"Maybe the Congressman I heard on that show the other day was right?" said Mark.

"What I don't know is if he knows we know he doesn't know what he's talking about?" mused Dante.

"Mr. Sebastian, we were in a casino last night watching football, don't worry I wasn't drinking, and this television ad came on just ripping the President."

"Dad, it was wild. They said he's lied about everything since he's been in office and he has no real plans for America since he's the *Misleader*. I think it's pretty cool we live in a country where you can say something like that about the guy at the top and still be alive. Try it in Iraq under Saddam and you'd be dead in a ditch somewhere before the commercial ended."

"Mark, I have to ask, did you guys ever start to question if you were doing the right thing over there?"

"No, Marines aren't trained to do that," explained Mark. "If you start to question the orders you're given then you dishonor the Corps, you start questioning what you're supposed to do, and the end result will probably be a lot of Marines getting killed. We can't go into battle not completely believing in what we're doing. Sure, some guys including me questioned why we still had to be there after the President landed on the aircraft carrier and said it was all over. Most of us thought it was pretty stupid when he made his *Bring them on* speech and then the bad guys brought it on us. I mean, it's easy for anyone to say anything when they're not getting shot at. But I don't really care if history shows our reasons for going to war turn out to be justified or not. It happened and we went over there and did exactly what we were told to do. It wasn't like we really had a choice in the matter."

"I'm not trying to upset you, Mark."

"I know, but I read newspapers and magazines, watch the tube and surf the internet for news," said Mark, somewhat defensively. "I know there's a lot of finger pointing and second-guessing going on, and maybe it's for good reason. If the Administration didn't tell us the truth when they sent us to war, then let the voters decide what to do about it in the next election. To tell you the truth, I don't really care much about the Administration, or the people of Iraq. All I care about is you, Mom, Emmy, Grandpa, Terri, and my Marines. My world can't get much better or simpler than that."

"Amen to that, son."

Terri gave his arm a loving squeeze.

*   *   *

The Marine Corps Ball in San Diego was held at a posh seaside resort and well-attended by handsome Marines young and old in full dress. They were accompanied by a bevy of elegantly dressed, well coiffed, bejeweled, exotically scented, and pointedly stunning women for an evening of spirited conversation, danceable music, fine food, ample drink, continual laughter, and intensely romantic eye contact on a crisp but clear early December evening.

On the dance floor Captain Dylan proudly twirled lovely Caressa about, Oliver Ralston boogied hard with his heavenly Sherry, Hilario Valdespino showed off some hot-blooded moves with his salsa partner Bettina, and Jimmy Sykes kept spinning his busty Becky around and around so he'd have the pleasure of catching her again. Mark danced with a thoroughly luscious Terri in close formation, his hand rarely moving from the area where the bare skin on the small of her back met the material covering her gloriously rounded lower torso.

Toward the end of the evening during a break in the music, Valdespino approached Mark as they were getting their drinks refilled. Valdespino motioned off to a corner where Captain Dylan and all the other company commanders were meeting with the Colonel himself. The discussions looked increasingly serious.

"I wonder what's going on?" asked Valdespino.

"Maybe the Colonel doesn't appreciate all the dirty dancing you've been doing?"

The Company Commanders saluted the Colonel as he walked away. The Captains summoned their Lieutenants, First Sergeants, and Staff Sergeants for a briefing, and they in turn soon scattered throughout the room to talk to their Marines.

Mark saw Captain Dylan motioning to Caressa that he had to go outside and holding up five fingers to let her know for how long. First Sergeant Ralston walked up to Sykes, said something quickly, and then moved onto the next Marine. Sykes nodded, shrugged over to Mark and Valdespino, and motioned for them to follow. Quickly all the Marines in the ballroom were leaving their dates and heading off to different locations outside in small groups.

Terri walked up next to Caressa, puzzled.

"What's going on?"

"I wish I knew..." replied a worried Caressa.

*   *   *

When all the Marines in Captain Dylan's company were assembled outside near the pool, the Captain took a moment to look over all the Marines proudly and then smiled.

"I don't know about all of you Marines, but when I look inside the ballroom and see all the beautiful women in there, I think we Hard Dogs might just be even more charming than we think we are!"

Laughs and *hoo-rahs* greeted the appraisal.

"The Colonel and I want to thank you all for coming," continued Captain Dylan. "We know there's some considerable expense involved and even if you hadn't been able to come tonight, none of your fellow Marines would've thought any less of you. Now to the business at hand...We could let you all go home tonight and receive news of your future in a few weeks, but we feel it would be remiss of us not to share what knowledge we have with you."

The Marines looked at each other expectantly.

"At the end of January you will return for active duty. For the next month we will undergo intensive specialized training. Sometime in early March we will be deployed back to Iraq once again."

Groans and a few mutterings of "Oh Shit!" and "Damn!" were heard and a lot of lumps in the throat were seen among the men; some of whom shook their heads or looked at each other with crestfallen eyes.

"Look, I know you're all brave men, I've seen it first-hand," nodded Captain Dylan a little solemnly. "It's not so much the job we have to do as much as it is leaving our parents, our children, and all those beautiful ladies inside. This is always the hardest part of military service and possibly the absolute worst part of war."

"Captain, do you know if we will be backing up Mortuary Affairs again?"

"I don't foresee us being a Force Support Group any more, Corporal Sykes. That particular MA unit is not scheduled for this rotation. All of the Colonel's companies are expected to be utilized as aggressive assault units. Marines are going to be responsible for cleaning up the Sunni Triangle so I expect us to be deployed somewhere in Al Anbar Province, which will include large cities such as Fallujah, Ramadi, and other areas of heightened resistance."

"Any idea how long we'll be there?"

"I don't have any visibility on that yet, Shark. Potentially for as long as they need us."

"I can't go back in there and tell my wife this."

"I'm not going to tell my lady either, Lance Corporal Valdespino," agreed Captain Dylan. "Go back in there with a smile, tell them the Colonel just wanted to thank us all, and when you're alone later tonight or tomorrow or next week or whenever the time seems right, tell them then. Hell, I'm as scared as you all are.

Not about the war in Iraq, but about relationships here at home. My wedding was just re-scheduled for April and now it's going to be canceled for the third time. If I tell Caressa about this right now, I'm afraid she might run out the front door crying and I might not ever see her again. So this is just as hard on me as it is on the rest of you. In any event, I'll look forward to seeing all of you back here in San Diego in about seven weeks. Expect a few promotions and medals to be awarded."

"Now, let's all go back in there before they become too suspicious. Be brave, and when you're alone tonight please remember the rule of engagement, wear protection as needed, and men...please exercise good trigger discipline. Good to go?"

*   *   *

In a partially darkened hotel room overlooking the ocean with the window shades open to the moonlight, Mark laid on the bed with Terri sprawled across him, her head and arm on his chest, and his arm around her. They were still dressed in the clothes they had worn to the ball, and their eyes showed where tears had been as they looked off into the future together.

"I don't know how I'm going to be able to tell my Mom and Dad," surmised Mark. "They both freaked out when I joined the Marines and then when I told them I was going to fight in Iraq I thought they were both going to have heart attacks. Now it's going to happen all over again, maybe only worse."

"I know exactly how they're going to feel."

Mark leaned over and kissed her forehead.

"I'm sorry you have to go through this too."

"You mean I still have some choice in the matter? Don't be sorry, Mark. I don't ever regret meeting you, or feeling the way I do."

"What planet are you from?"

"Mark's…It's right next to Mars."

"You're funny..."

"It helps to try and be sometimes."

"Life is funny. I used to rely on Angelo to prop me up and then he was gone," reflected Mark.. "Then I met you and my whole world seemed to instantly change when I saw something in you. We've been together the last week having more fun than I thought I could ever imagine, and here it is the first night we're really alone together, and I'm lying here on a bed crying with no romantic energy whatsoever."

"That's all right. Maybe you had a little too much of that energy to begin with?"

"All of this is Angelo's doing, like a curse."

"What do you mean?"

"When Angelo was telling me about you and I was wondering how this totally cocky guy could be so lucky and where the hell my Terri was, one of the things he kept saying to me was that you weren't just a girl a guy dates, you're a woman a man marries."

"Angelo said that? Oh my God…"

"He was right. When you took my arm and we went into Angelo's house the first time we met, I knew right then and there I was either going to marry you or die trying. Terri, I don't want to just make love to you tonight; I want to make love to you every night. This is the only way it could ever possibly be enough."

Terri moved so their eyes were inches apart.

"What is it you're really saying here, Mark? You have said you love me and I've said that I love you. Your Grandpa took care of clearing all of that up. Do you want to marry me before we make love?"

"All I know is, I want to marry you someday."

"But not before you're re-deployed?"

"No, If Captain Dylan has to wait until he gets back, then maybe so can I. As long as I know you'll at least consider it, we could at least be planning a future together. I don't want our parents freaking out because they think we're rushing into something. We've only really known each other less than two months but I do know what I want, and what I want is you."

"Sounds reasonable. I've considered it carefully, Mark, and this is something I definitely want to do."

"You want to marry me?"

"Yes, I'd like to do that too," she smiled, leaning forward to kiss him. "But for now, this will just have to do. Don't worry, I'll be gentle with you…"

Lips and bodies came together as naturally as the ocean waves crashing the shore outside.

* * *

MARK'S JOURNAL:

Hey Terri:
Are you surprised that my last entry into this journal is addressed to you? You told me you'd like to read it sometime and as much as it initially scared me, it does make sense. I don't want to have any secrets from you, except unless I surprise you with something nice.

There are pages I contemplated destroying, but as embarrassing as it might be for me to have someone else read some of the things I've written, the fact remains I expressed a real part of me and you should know as much as you can possibly tolerate if you're thinking about spending the rest of our lives together.

As for the anger stuff, my Dad says it's all right for Dr. Jekyll to have Mr. Hyde locked up in the closet as long as the doctor has the key and not the patient. As for the sex related stuff, I'm glad I'm not Angelo or the entry would be longer and far more embarrassing. I do know the difference between sex and love and have you to thank for very gently teaching me the difference in a way which I will never forget.

I know you and the rest of my family are trying very hard not to show how worried you all must be about me having to go back over to Iraq. It's not like I really have any choice so I'm just going to make the best of it. I'll be smart, keep my head down, and try not to do anything stupid. What I will do is keep my eye on the prize, because now I really do have a future to dream about and come home to. You will be my breath of life and something special which keeps me alive.

So try not to worry about me being gone too much. Love will bring us back together into a future I see as being so bright it will put all of the sacrifices to get there behind us. The fact is, my beautiful wife to be someday, this journal is yours now just as much as it is mine. Read it from the back to the front so you can see where I am now, before you find out how far you've helped me come from. When I wrote in my journal before, it was because I needed someone to talk to and I only trusted my own self to understand. Now I have a best friend whom I love and can see in the mirror when I look at myself. From now on when I need to open my heart, the words and emotions I feel and need to express will be directed at you.

I love you, baby. Mark

* * *

Chef Dante found him in the cooler.

"Dudley…"

"What now, Chef?" the Assistant Executive Chef sighed as he rotated meat and fish in the cooler.

"How are you doing?"

"Fine I guess, considering…"

"Considering you're overworked, underpaid and have two kids and a wife and an ex-wife to support?"

"Yeah, that's part of it."

"I guess the rest is my fault."

"I didn't say that, Chef."

"I understand, Dudley. It actually makes what I have to tell you much easier."

Dudley turned to face him, fearing the worst.

"So, it's finally come to this, letting me go."

"No, I'm letting myself go," announced Dante. "I turned in my resignation this morning."

"Don't screw with me, Chef." pleaded Dudley. "It's been one of those incredibly hairy weeks!"

"I'm serious. I just left the Director's office."

Dudley suddenly realized his boss was indeed serious. "You're not leaving because of me, are you?"

"No, I'm leaving because of me."

Dudley was silent while all the ramifications began filtering through his head. He turned and grabbed Dante with both arms, beseeching him.

"You can't do this to me, Chef! If you leave and they hire someone else, there's no way they'll understand the way I am like you do! I'll be out the door before I even know it!"

"Relax, Dudley. No one wants to get rid of you. I submitted an exit plan for me to turn over all operations to you for the next thirty days while I'm here. I'm confident management will buy into my

181

proposal to have you take over, since they are sold on the fact you've virtually been running this place by yourself for a long time."

"Not true, Chef. I defer everything to you."

"Look, do you want a chance at this job or not?"

Reality hit Dudley like a sack of potatoes. He sank to the floor in shock, with his head resting on a box of salmon filets. Then a light came on inside him.

"You're right! Hell yes, I can do this! The stewards like me, the sous chefs and cooks put up with me, and management is fairly cool. The only person I wasn't sure about …was you?"

"No, the only person you weren't sure about is yourself. Some of us generals can be pretty tough, Dudley. But we know when it's time to retire from the battle, and that's when we want to and not when someone else demands it. Remember that."

"What are you going to do?" asked Dudley.

"Stephanie and I are going to be married. We'd like you and your wife to attend."

"Wow…that was really quick!"

"We've been dating almost a year."

"Oh, where was I?" asked Dudley.

"Only time will tell. We'll be in Italy during February. When we get back I'm going to take some time off, maybe write a cookbook or something while Mark is overseas again. Then, who knows?"

"Chef, do you really think I'm ready for this?"

"No, but we have thirty days to create a total confidence makeover," surmised Dante, half in jest. "So the sooner we get started, the better!"

*　*　*

"Emmy, Terri got accepted at UNLV."

"Great! So what's the problem?"

"I want her to stay at our house while I'm overseas since it's kind of like my headquarters and I want everyone to be there."

"So I repeat, what's the problem?"

"Well, theoretically at least, it is Dad's house."

"Mark, we all love Terri. Not just because of what she means to you, but because of who she is. Leave it to me, I'll take care of all the details."

"Cool, thanks!"

"Hey, Dad is planning to pop the question to Stephanie on Christmas day. If she says yes, as Las Vegas odds makers are betting, he wants to get married before you deploy so you can be his best man."

* * *

In the living room of the Cicci home in Chicago, Mark found a seat on the couch between Terri and Mrs. Cicci as the program started on the wide screen television in front of them. A huge Christmas tree was behind them in one corner of the room, and Terri's parents joined other expectant members of the Cicci family, including Nonna, to watch the broadcast.

Diana Scott's smiling image filled the screen.

"Good evening and Merry Christmas. This is Diana Scott and welcome to a special edition of 'Three Voices' where tonight we continue to examine the effect the war in Iraq has had on the families of some of the young Americans who have served there."

The camera pulled back to show three other people sitting at the table with Diana Scott. Cheers went up through the room as first Dante Sebastian and then

Frank Cicci came into view. Also at the table was an equally somber middle-aged black woman.

"Joining us, first to my left is Estelle Cantrell from Atlanta, whose son Jason served in the Army in Iraq. On my right is Mr. Frank Cicci from Chicago and Chef Dante Sebastian from Las Vegas, whose sons both served in the same Marine unit in Iraq. Welcome to all of you and thank you for spending part of your holiday with us. Mr. Cicci, let's start with you…"

"Thank you for having us, Miss Scott," nodded Frank Cicci as the camera panned in, drawing another chorus of cheers from the Cicci living room in Chicago. "Please, call me Frank."

"Very well, Frank, Several weeks ago you wrote a very impassioned letter which was published in a Chicago newspaper and has since garnered some national attention. In it you spoke of how the death of your youngest son Angelo in combat this fall has left such a deep emotional scar over your entire family that this holiday season, and perhaps for many years to come, will, as I quote from the article 'ring forth a hollow note of joy in the emptiness of our hearts'. How difficult has this been for you and your family?"

Frank Cicci's face filled the screen as the camera came in close. A tear rolled down one cheek and he wiped it away, quickly composing himself. Those watching him in the Cicci living room had more difficulty keeping themselves composed.

"The death of my son was a tragedy, but his life was never a tragedy," pointed out Frank Cicci. "This is what makes this first holiday season without him so painful for us all. My son has always been the penultimate life of the party for our family, and a very big family it is. From the time he was just a little boy he was always there to cheer everyone up who was down and pump up the laughter and excitement when we all got together. To his relatives he was not only beloved, but treasured. That energy isn't there anymore, the joy certainly isn't palpable, and I hope for the sake of my family it won't somehow be irreplaceable."

Diana Scott commiserated.

"Mrs. Cantrell, how is your son Jason doing and where is he right now?"

"My boy, well, Jason he's doing as best as can be expected," she nodded slowly. "Right now he's at Walter Reed Hospital near Washington, where we expect him to be for a good while longer. My daughters and his youngest brother and I just left him yesterday. He seemed to be in good spirits. We brought him one of those video game machines he likes."

"What happened to your son in Iraq?"

"From what I've been told, Miss Scott," said Estelle Cantrell, "my son and some other soldiers were on a patrol in Northern Iraq last summer when the enemy fired one of those rocket propelled grenades at the vehicle they were riding in. One of the boys was killed and my Jason got hurt pretty bad. Lost both his legs below the knees and his left hand, and there are other complications like the burns on his face. But we just have to thank the Good Lord he's still alive."

"What has this holiday season been like for your family?" asked Diana Scott gently.

"Very different, as you might imagine. You see, before my son went into the Army he was a very good basketball player in high school. Since he didn't have good enough grades to get a college scholarship his plan when he got out of the Army was to go back to college, get a good education and try to make the team on his own. But now he's nineteen years old and the only way he's ever going to play basketball again is in a wheelchair. Now, I have faith when his heart and mind grow strong enough he'll will his body to do just it, but it's still very hard for all of us to see him the way he is now, knowing many of his dreams have died and he is going to have to fight uphill against great odds to find another dream he can live with again. We pray each and every day that he can and will accomplish this."

"Thank you, Mrs. Cantrell. Now on to Dante Sebastian, whose holiday has been different from our other guests. Mr. Sebastian?"

"It has been very different, Miss Scott," began Dante, looking a little nervous before the cameras and under the bright lights. "My son Mark came home relatively unscathed physically, but emotionally I think what he witnessed over in Iraq will stay with him for a long time. Frank's son Angelo was Mark's best friend and Mark was actually driving the Humvee on the day it was hit by an IED, an Improvised Explosive Device roadside bomb. Angelo was killed instantly by the blast, while my son only suffered a few cuts and bruises and a slight concussion. The line between joy and sorrow, life and death, and exhilaration and devastation, is indeed a very fine one when your children are sent to Iraq."

"How has your son reacted to being home?"

"It took some adjusting for him, mainly because of what he'd experienced with Angelo," related Dante," but I'm proud of the way he's got himself back into a good place again. He met a wonderful girl, fell in love, and I'm very happy for both of them. All in all, he's back to being just plain old Mark, which to me is a very good thing. Right now, if I'm not mistaken, my son is sitting in Frank's living room in Chicago with his girlfriend and family members, watching this program and hoping I won't say something to embarrass him."

"I'm glad everything is going rather well now for you and your family," smiled Diana Scott.

"It is right now, but the holidays will end soon, a new year will start, and any joy we've had will be tempered by the fact my son just received orders to be re-deployed back to Iraq in a few months. The situation is just getting worse in Iraq and when the government sends your children over there to fight the wars they start, there's no guarantee our young men and women are going to come back alive or without permanent disabilities. So yes, we're happy he made it home alive, but for our family and many others a long nightmare is about to begin all over again."

At the Cicci residence, Mark shook his head while holding it in his hands. Terri shared his father's concern and looked to her own parents for support.

"Obviously, terrible news for your family, Mr. Sebastian," said Diana Scott. "Let me ask you all this: With the presidential election season heading into high gear with the upcoming primaries, what effect will the experiences of your sons in Iraq have upon how you see yourselves voting in the next election? Frank Cicci?"

"A very relevant question, Miss Scott," began Frank Cicci, thinking it over, "and also very difficult to answer. For me, it's a bit of a quandary since I'm a lifelong Republican and I've been successful enough in my business to have made significant contributions to the party. But lately, and this was even before Angelo died, I've been troubled by the direction our party leadership has taken. I'm reading how the so-called *facts* used in convincing Congress to authorize going to war in Iraq were distorted, and there may in fact be a cover-up going on to hide those apparent lies. This troubles me. Then I read how it's no coincidence the President assembled a war team when he got into office and we wound up fighting in Iraq since this Administration was apparently planning for war in Iraq even before 9/11 happened. Again, this is very troubling. Of course, the Administration will deny it all. I do support the war on terror, but I thought it was going to be centered on Osama bin Laden and Al Qaeda in Afghanistan? All these developments are beginning to lead me to seriously question why our direction has morphed into something else completely, and what in fact my son really died for?"

"Serious concerns, indeed," agreed Diana Scott. "Estelle Cantrell, how about you?"

"Unlike Mr. Cicci, more often than not I have voted for Democrats," explained Mrs. Cantrell, "partly because they seem to be more responsive to the needs of the black community. Some folks claim this President may have stolen the last election, and maybe he did, but you have to expect those kinds of things in elections when the political system is all probably corrupt anyway. But I also believe when the smoke clears all Americans have to support whatever leader we wind up with. Once they're in power they're probably not going to do what we want them to, or what they promised to do, so all we can really do is have faith that our Lord's will prevails for us in the end."

"How do you think your son will vote, and will it influence your own decision in any way?"

"You know, it's funny Miss Scott, but my boy, even after everything which has happened to him and everything he's going to have to continue to go through, he still supports the war and the president. Isn't that something? My daughter Charmaine, who is just a year younger than Jason and very close to him, asked him just the other day if he regretted going to Iraq. You know what he told her? He said he regretted what happened to him over there, but not the fact he went. If voters decide we need new leaders to take the country in a different direction, how will it change what happened to Mr. Cicci's son or my son? It won't."

"Thank you, Mrs. Cantrell. Mr. Sebastian?"

In the Cicci living room, Mark briefly covered his head again, almost afraid to watch.

"I totally do understand where Mrs. Cantrell is coming from," replied Dante. "I think my son feels much the same way and I would hate to see him going back to Iraq if he didn't believe in himself or what he was doing. But how I see it from my perspective is this is simply the Administration's war, not America's. The war hawks in Washington are the ones waging this war and America is going to be left to clean up the financial mess, as well as paying for it with the blood of our own children. Since we live in a country still in fear after 9/11, the Democrats may not have the guts in 2004 to stand up firmly to the president on this war. If they fail to do so, then the election might get stolen again and mark my words, in 2008 we'll still be up to our ears in the chaos of Iraq with no end in sight unless there's a profound change in Washington."

"So you don't hold any hope our military leaders will be able to turn around the now quickly eroding security situation in Iraq, Mr. Sebastian?"

"None whatsoever, and it has as much to do with the sectarian religious divide within Iraq as it has to do with basic human nature. The Sunni and Shiite people hate each other and have been at war for thousands of years. Simply getting rid of Saddam Hussein will not solve the root problem. At the very least it will just lead to a fierce civil war in Iraq we will be unable to control. Secondly, as it is now being spun, we have apparently replaced a tyrannical dictator in the cause of democracy. The Shiites approve but the Sunnis don't. But what they both do agree on is not allowing the so-called liberators to stick around as an occupying force. In the end, despite their deep religious and political differences the Sunnis and Shiites will come together to fight against a common enemy… us."

"Dante and I talked about this on the plane coming over," interjected Frank Cicci. "This is the analogy I came up with. Say another country more powerful than us invades to liberate the country from a tyrannical rule or a bad president, or whatever they don't like. But instead of liberating us and leaving, they decide to stay since they don't trust us to not let whatever has happened, to ever happen again."

"In this type of scenario," continued Dante, "every able-bodied man, woman, and child in this country would rise up and do whatever they could to expel the invaders. This is basic human nature on a purely nationalistic level. The people of a sovereign nation would never give up this fight and if they died doing so, more of their children and brothers and sisters would replace them and both their cause and their will would strengthen into such a force the invaders would have no recourse but to cut losses and leave."

"We're really not a nation which believes in cut and run," continued Frank, "but if we shouldn't have been there in the first place, maybe we should just swallow some humble pie and make a law so we don't allow ourselves or our leaders to put us all in this most vulnerable position again."

"Exactly!" agreed Dante. "Our leaders don't seem to see this cycle developing in Iraq, and that they aren't prepared for the obvious consequences is both a very frightening and-"

"-a very regrettable and totally unexplainable mystery to us all," concluded Frank Cicci.

"But what do I know? I'm just a chef..."

"And I am but a humble mortician,"

"I manage a credit union," offered Estelle.

"If you're not careful, you all might just wind up being regular panelists on this show," smiled Diana Scott, very pleased how the show wrapped up. "Next week on 'Three Voices' an all new set of panelists will start debating the upcoming 2004 presidential election season. Estelle Cantrell, Frank Cicci, Dante Sebastian, thank you all so very much for sharing your incisive thoughts and family insights with us during this war time holiday season. Merry Christmas, America. We wish you all a safe and pleasant good night."

Applause filled the Cicci living room and Mark had to nod in agreement with the positive performance of the neophyte panelists.

"Dads rocked the house!" beamed Terri.

"They did all right. Guess I'll keep mine."

* * *

Military helicopters buzzed over the Las Vegas Strip to deter any terrorist activities as three hundred thousand celebrants braved the last chilly night of the year in good spirits, most of it of the liquid variety.

"The thing about New Years which has always really appealed to me," smiled a re-invigorated Dudley in his new Executive Chef's coat with an arm around his current wife, "is it doesn't matter what we've done the year before, whether good, bad, ugly, or otherwise. We are now presented with a new year to forget what we've done, ascend to new heights, plan for a better future, or maybe just do nothing at all."

"Here's to America!" toasted Grandpa Marcus happily while almost breaking Dudley's glass with his.

"I would like to propose a toast to the memory of a brave Marine, Angelo Cicci, who brightened his family's lives for twenty loving years," offered Dante

Cheers went up and drinks went down as everyone awaited the coming fireworks. Mark and Terri shared a railing together.

"How would Angelo feel about you and me?"

"I don't think he'd have a problem with us being together. Angelo had wild oats to sow that might have lasted him a lifetime. You and I falling in love might have been the best thing to happen to him. That way we would all still be a part of the same family."

"He'll always be with us."

"Absolutely...."

"Son..."

"Hey, Dad dude, what's up?"

"Remember the pact we made last year?"

"Yes I do, and am proud to have fulfilled it."

"Will you agree to the same terms again?"

"Absolutely," agreed Mark, "It looks like we might be in Iraq for six months to a year. So if by chance I don't make it back home by the 4th of July, save me a few sparklers and beers, okay? I do know the way home, and I will definitely be coming back alive."

"You're sure a lot stronger and braver than I could ever hope to be, Mark," admired Dante, first hugging him and then Terri. "While I'm sure being a Marine has a lot to do with all of this, I like to think this young lady here is at least partly responsible for it."

"We'll keep a real close eye on her while you're gone," Stephanie assured Mark.

"I really appreciate it. After all, she's been very gentle with me," mused Mark, getting a playful nudge from Terri in the process.

"That can change very quickly if you're not careful," she reminded him with a veiled whisper.

Emmy stepped to the forefront and clinked two glasses together to address the revelers.

"A final toast for this year and a first toast to the New Year," proposed Emmy loudly as the countdown to a New Year began. "To this I quote Pink Floyd…"

"Long we live and high we fly, smiles we'll give and tears we'll cry. All we touch and all we see, is all our lives will ever be."

"HOO-RAH!" shouted out Mark and Grandpa Marcus as the fireworks began for yet another year.

The End

Steven Graham Charles was born in Northern California, the son of a portrait artist and a radio personality. He began writing early in life, but not until young daughter Dyana asked what was happening in the bright stars above them one crystal clear night in a small Northern California town, did he start writing fiction. That is how Stars In The Wind began, circa 1976.

The author hopes his research driven non-fiction works will prove to be progressive, creative, and confrontational; such as political conflicts in the present world would seem to demand. With fictional stories, the author writes in a cinematic style best suitable for movie adaptation. A 100 to 120 page story may seem short, but results in an up to two hour movie as in most screenplays one page equates to one minute in a movie. Writing in a cinematic style essentially means novelizing screenplays, where the story is told only through location, action, and dialogue. Anything else revealed must be shown on the page in order to be seen on the screen. These books are meant to be movies for the mind.

The author does not prescribe to following one particular writing genre, the argument being all stories really contain the same elements of exposition, conflict, humor, romance, philosophy, tragedy, and resolution. It doesn't matter if it is a western, a medieval journey, a political thriller, science fiction and fantasy, military affairs, romantic drama, or any other genre. In the end, story structure principally remains the same regardless of what diverse genre is involved.

The author's literary collection is available from Amazon for readers, bookstores, and producers.